W9-CAL-125

Enjoy all of these American Girl Mysteries®:

THE SILENT STRANGER   A *Kaya* Mystery

LADY MARGARET'S GHOST   A *Felicity* Mystery

SECRETS IN THE HILLS   A *Josefina* Mystery

THE RUNAWAY FRIEND   A *Kirsten* Mystery

SHADOWS ON SOCIETY HILL   An *Addy* Mystery

THE CRY OF THE LOON   A *Samantha* Mystery

SECRETS AT CAMP NOKOMIS   A *Rebecca* Mystery

MISSING GRACE   A *Kit* Mystery

CLUES IN THE SHADOWS   A *Molly* Mystery

THE TANGLED WEB   A *Julie* Mystery

and many more!

— A *Julie* MYSTERY —

THE PUZZLE OF THE PAPER DAUGHTER

by Kathryn Reiss

⭐ American Girl®

Published by American Girl Publishing, Inc.
Copyright © 2010 by American Girl, LLC
All rights reserved. No part of this book may be used
or reproduced in any manner whatsoever without written
permission except in the case of brief quotations embodied
in critical articles and reviews.

Questions or comments? Call 1-800-845-0005, visit our
Web site at **americangirl.com**, or write to Customer Service,
American Girl, 8400 Fairway Place, Middleton, WI 53562-0497.

Printed in China
10 11 12 13 14 15 LEO 10 9 8 7 6 5 4 3 2 1

All American Girl marks, American Girl Mysteries®, Julie™, Julie Albright™,
Ivy™, and Ivy Ling™ are trademarks of American Girl, LLC.

The characters and events portrayed in this book are fictitious. Any similarity
to real persons, living or dead, is coincidental and not intended.

PICTURE CREDITS
The following individuals and organizations have generously
given permission to reprint illustrations contained in "Looking Back":
pp. 174–175—two young immigrant women, courtesy of California State
Parks, 2010; poem tiles, Justin Sullivan/Getty Images News/Getty Images;
pp. 176–177—toddlers, courtesy of California State Parks, 2010; railroad
laborers, Pajero Valley Historical Association; pp. 178–179—Chinese
immigrant family, courtesy of the California History Room, California State
Library, Sacramento, California; identity card and coaching notes, courtesy
of the Museum of Chinese in America (MoCA); pp. 180–181—Angel Island
detention room, California Historical Society, FN-I8240/CHS2009.09I.tif;
barracks interior, photo by Kathryn Reiss, printed with permission of California
State Parks; Angel Island detainees outdoors, courtesy of California State Parks,
2010; pp. 182–183—poem inscribed on wall, photo by Kathryn Reiss, printed
with permission of California State Parks; former detainee
touring restored barracks and Angel Island today,
Justin Sullivan/Getty Images News/Getty Images.

Illustrations by Jean-Paul Tibbles

With gratitude to Judy Yung, PhD,
for her assistance on Chinese history and culture

Cataloging-in-Publication Data
available from the Library of Congress.

To Anna-Kristina Moseidjord,
a very good writer
and a very special friend—
with love

TABLE OF CONTENTS

1
SURPRISES

Julie Albright and her older sister, Tracy, sat at the kitchen table after school, munching chocolate chip cookies and chatting about the upcoming Valentine Disco. The telephone on the wall jangled, and Julie reached over to grab the receiver.

"Hi, honey," said Mom. "Would you and Tracy please come down and help me out here? I've got some new bags of clothing that need sorting, but the shop is full of customers. I'm swamped!"

Julie's mother's shop, Gladrags, was on the first floor of their apartment building. Gladrags sold all sorts of fascinating and funky clothing and handmade jewelry, candles, and housewares. Julie felt proud of the way her mom could take old dresses or pairs of secondhand jeans and refurbish them into really cool, trendy outfits and handbags. These days, the shop was so busy that Mom asked the girls to help out more and more often. Sixteen-year-old Tracy already worked for pay every other Saturday, and now their mother was talking about hiring more help.

"We'll be right down," Julie said.

Inside Gladrags, Mom looked up from the sales counter with a smile. "Ivy's grandmother dropped these off this morning," she said, holding out two large plastic bags full of clothing. "She said she and her neighbors had been doing some cleaning in preparation for Chinese New Year."

Ivy Ling had been Julie's best friend since they were little girls. Ivy's grandmother, Po Po, and grandfather, Gung Gung, owned a restaurant, The Happy Panda, in San Francisco's Chinatown not far from where Julie used to live. Now, since her parents' divorce, only Julie's dad lived in that house, right across the street from Ivy's house. Mr. Albright was often away because his job as an airline pilot kept him traveling. But whenever he was home, Julie and Tracy spent the weekend with him. Julie was glad she and Ivy could get together whenever she was in the old neighborhood to spend time with Dad.

Julie opened one of the bags her mom had handed her and peeked inside. The folded garments looked old and worn, but Julie knew Mom would turn them into something cool and stylish.

"Be sure to check all the garments for tears," said Mom. "I'll need to make any repairs before I add appliqués and beads. And please set aside any red or pink garments for my Valentine's Day display."

"Oh, Mom—that reminds me," said Tracy, turning back eagerly. "The disco club at school is organizing a Valentine's Day dance for families and friends. It'll be held in the high school gym. The club will teach everyone the latest moves—it's going to be a blast! I'm on the decorating committee."

"Tracy was just telling me about it," Julie added. "I definitely want to go."

"Sounds fun," said Mom.

"Can I invite Ivy?" asked Julie.

"The more the merrier," said Tracy, grinning. "It's a fund-raiser to help support a shelter for homeless teens."

Julie spun across the shop in what she imagined was a cool disco move. It would be so fun to go to a dance!

"Whoa, watch the candle display!" Mrs. Albright cautioned as Julie knocked into a shelf. "Wait till you're at the dance before you start whirling— Oh, excuse me a minute." She turned away to answer the phone. "Hello, Gladrags. How may I help you?"

Tracy picked up her bag of clothing and headed for the stairs. But Julie lingered, noticing Mom's exasperated expression as she listened to the voice on the phone.

"Oh, Olivia!" Mom said into the receiver. "I'd *love* to talk, but I'm at work now and it's busy... What? Yes, yes, of course... Oh dear. Oh no..."

Mom looked back at Julie and winked.

Julie stifled a giggle. Olivia Kaminsky was an old childhood friend of her mom's. She lived far away in Virginia, and she phoned now and then and talked Mom's ears off in a booming voice. Julie looked at the line of customers waiting to make their purchases and gave her mom a sympathetic glance. Then she picked up her bag of clothing and followed Tracy upstairs.

Back in the apartment, the girls sat down together and started sorting through the clothes from Ivy's grandmother.

"Hey, I call the silk pants," Julie said after a moment. "I'm going to ask Mom to show me how to make them into one of those shoulder bags with the fringe."

"Cool," said Tracy absently. She was trying on a pair of shiny red high-heeled shoes. "Look at these—they'd be perfect for the disco!" Then she sighed. "But they're miles too small." She put them aside for the Valentine's display.

The girls piled the red and pink clothing on the table. There was a pink cotton nightgown, a man's gray woolen vest with a red satin lining, a floor-length red sequined gown, and a red quilted coat, as well as the red high heels.

"I call the ball gown, too!" said Julie, grabbing the long dress. She pirouetted, holding the silky dress up by its skinny straps. "Wouldn't this look great at the disco? I'd really stand out."

"You sure would," said Tracy drily, "because everyone else will be wearing jeans!"

Julie sighed. *What's the point of having a dance if you can't even dress up for it?* She folded the red dress regretfully.

Then she reached for the red quilted coat. Sticking her hands into each of the deep pockets on the front, she wiggled her fingers, searching for tears that would need mending. Sure enough, she found a little rip in the seam of one pocket. Something rustled as she withdrew her fingers. Exploring more deeply, she felt a small folded piece of paper caught in the lining. Carefully she drew it out.

"Hey, look!" Julie held up the folded square for Tracy to see. "A letter." She unfolded the paper. "Oh, wait—it's in Chinese. At least I think it is."

Tracy looked at the page and nodded. "Looks like it. Well, no surprise there, since it came from Chinatown."

"True..." Julie squinted down at the paper in her hand. "Wow, it's like someone tried to cram words onto every possible space."

"Someone had a lot to say," laughed Tracy. "And not a lot of paper. Maybe it's an old fortune from a fortune cookie!"

"No, it's too long for that." Julie fingered the yellowed edges of the thin rice paper. "It looks old." The tiny handwritten Chinese characters crisscrossed the page, crowding into the corners. A little prick of excitement tingled along Julie's shoulder blades. "I wonder what it says."

"*You will travel far and wide,*" Tracy pretended to translate. "*But before you go, you will give all your allowance to your wise and worthy older sister.*"

Julie gave her a withering look just as Mrs. Albright opened the door. "Look, Mom," Julie said eagerly, holding out the note. "I found it inside the lining of this red jacket."

"You will be a generous sister and sort the rest of these clothes by yourself," Tracy intoned.

Mrs. Albright glanced at the paper. "Most likely an old shopping list or something," she replied, heading to the sink to wash her hands. She opened the refrigerator and peered inside. "Hmm, it looks like *I* need to make a shopping list. Good thing you girls will be eating with your dad tonight. I'll just have leftovers."

Julie was still examining the note. "I don't know. I suppose it *could* be a grocery list. But it's a pretty long one."

"Maybe they had a big family," Tracy pointed out. "Or friends coming for dinner."

"While we're on the subject of friends," said Mom, "I had a call from Olivia. She's moving here to San Francisco!"

"Oh, that'll be nice for you," said Julie.

"She's been taking care of her father for years," Mom continued, "but now that he's gone to live with her brother, Olivia is ready for a change. She says she wants to start over somewhere new. She'd like to live where she already knows someone—so she's coming here to look for a job."

"Great," said Tracy disinterestedly.

"Hey, why not hire her to work at Gladrags?" suggested Julie. "You know you need more help."

Mom smiled at Julie. "That's exactly what I told her, and she jumped at the chance. The thing is, though, that the pay for a part-time job won't be enough for her to live on. She'll need a second job—or a full-time job eventually—to be able to afford an apartment of her own. So in the meantime..."

Tracy's disinterest vanished. "In the mean-time, *what?*" she asked pointedly.

"In the meantime, she'll move in with us."

"Here?" Julie stared at her mom, all thought of the Chinese note momentarily forgotten. "But we don't have room for anyone else."

"All the bedrooms are taken," Tracy con-curred, frowning.

"We'll make room," Mom said firmly. "It

won't be for long. Just a month or two while she learns her way around the city and finds a job that will pay the rent."

Julie's heart sank. "And . . . where will she sleep?" The living room couch was only a love seat—not long enough for a grown-up to stretch out fully.

"She'll sleep in your room, honey." Mom walked over and squeezed Julie's shoulders. "And you'll move in with Tracy. Her room is bigger, so the sleepover mattress will fit just fine. The two of you can be roommates for a while."

"But Mom!" wailed Tracy.

Julie didn't wail or fuss. Tracy was melodramatic enough for both of them, and besides, Julie knew there was no point. Mom's mind was made up, and she'd already issued the invitation to her old friend. Probably Olivia Kaminsky was packing her suitcase this very minute, eager to fly out to San Francisco and into Julie's bedroom.

"I'm sorry, girls. Olivia really needs a place to stay, and she's my oldest childhood friend.

When she asked if she could come to us, I had to say yes. It'll work out, you'll see."

"There'll be no peace and quiet," grumbled Tracy. "She's such a chatterbox."

"She'll be working at Gladrags or searching for jobs most of the time," Mom reassured Tracy.

"There'll be no *room*," muttered Tracy. "We'll have no privacy."

"Listen, girls, I expect both of you to be welcoming. All sorts of things can happen in people's lives to make them relocate. And if they come our way, the right thing to do is to *make* room." Then Mom smiled. "Olivia will be busy. You'll hardly know she's here."

Julie thought *that* was unlikely. Sleeping on the floor in Tracy's room, Julie would definitely know that Olivia Kaminsky was here.

"Maybe I can stay with Dad," she suggested.

Mrs. Albright shook her head. "With his flight schedule, he's gone half the time. And speaking of your dad, he'll be here soon. You girls had better get packed." She gave Julie's shoulders another squeeze. "Why not show your

Chinese letter to Ivy? Maybe someone in her family can read it."

Julie shrugged. But she folded the brittle square of paper and put it carefully into the pocket of her jeans. She would certainly be talking to her best friend—and about more than just the note.

Tracy leaned over and spoke in a dramatic voice full of doom. *"You will soon receive room-stealing visitor from far away."*

"It's not funny," Julie snapped. She grabbed the red coat and went to her bedroom. She pushed through the beaded curtain and stood in the doorway, looking around at all her dear, familiar things: her books and dolls lined up on the shelves, her India-print bedspread, her fuzzy rug in the shape of a bare foot next to the bed. She didn't want to leave them here for Olivia Kaminsky. And she didn't want to sleep in Tracy's bedroom any more than Tracy wanted her there.

Sighing, Julie stood in front of her mirror and tried on the red jacket. It was too tight in the shoulders and too short in the arms. Ivy's grandmother and many of her friends were shorter than Julie; maybe the jacket had belonged to one of them.

She pulled the folded rice paper from her pocket again and stared down at the tiny Chinese characters. Some of the lines were a bit shaky, as if the hand that wrote them had trembled. In fact, there was a strange feeling of urgency in the writing, Julie thought—as if the person who wrote the note had been tense or anxious.

Could it be a note from a friend, asking for help? Or maybe it was something for school. Maybe a child had been cramming for a test, taking notes. For Julie's last history test, her teacher had told the class they could each use one index card full of notes. She and her friend Joy had written on both sides of their cards in their smallest printing. Their friend T. J. had joked that they'd need a magnifying glass to read their notes. Julie had discovered that just writing down the dates and details of the historic events on her card the night before the test made it easy to remember them when she was taking the test the next afternoon. She hadn't even needed to look at her note card!

Well, she thought, folding up the paper and sticking it in the pocket of her jeans, *this note— whatever it says—is so old, it can't possibly matter anymore.* Still, she hoped the kid who'd written it at least got a good grade on the test.

Julie packed her overnight bag. She scooped up the doll she always slept with, Yue Yan— a gift from her best friend, Ivy—and slid her into the zippered side pocket. Then she sat looking out the window, waiting for Dad and trying not to think about Olivia Kaminsky.

2

PUZZLE FROM THE PAST

From the window, Julie finally saw her dad's blue car pull up. With a glad heart, she ran to open the door for him.

Dad hugged Julie and Tracy and apologized for being late. His flight had been delayed, he explained, as he led the girls out to the car.

Tracy sat in the front seat and launched into complaints about Mom's upcoming visitor, while Julie stowed her overnight bag in the backseat and then climbed in beside it. She stared out at the darkening street.

"Just before I left to come get you, the Lings phoned and asked if we'd like to join them for a meal at the Happy Panda tonight," Dad said, catching Julie's eye in the rearview mirror. "What do you say?"

"Sure!" said Julie, sitting up straight. Suddenly she didn't feel quite so bleak.

"Sounds good to me," Tracy agreed. "I love their wontons. And no dishes to wash up afterward."

"And I can ask Ivy to translate the note!" said Julie. She told Dad about finding the folded Chinese note in the lining of the red jacket.

"How intriguing," Dad said. "Maybe it will direct you to a treasure!"

Julie rolled her eyes. Dad could be so corny.

"Beautiful older sister will soon meet handsome stranger and get a date to the Valentine Disco," Tracy intoned as they pulled up near the Happy Panda. "That's what it says!"

❀

As they entered the restaurant, Julie sniffed appreciatively. The aromas of sizzling garlic, lemon, and ginger scented the air. The room hummed with the conversations of dozens of families savoring their meals. The walls of the restaurant were hung with colorful silk banners. Carved wooden screens separated the large room into cozy, intimate areas.

Ivy's grandparents, Po Po and Gung Gung, were bustling around, supervising the busy dining room. "So happy to see you!" they said to Julie's family.

Ivy's family had also just arrived. They were being seated at a large round table in the center of the room. Ivy's parents beckoned the Albrights to join them and greeted Julie's family warmly.

Julie gave Ivy a hug. "Hey, Poison Ivy!"

"Hey, Alley Oop!" Ivy hugged Julie back.

Ivy's twelve-year-old brother, Andrew, waved at Julie from the next table. Helium balloons were tied to the back of each chair at that table. Ivy explained that Andrew had been invited to a birthday dinner for his friend, Paul Chan. Paul was the son of Mrs. Chan, who taught the Saturday morning Chinese school that Andrew and Ivy both attended. Andrew would be spending the night at Paul's house with the other boys, but Ivy was going to sleep right here, at their grandparents' apartment above the restaurant.

"It's always easier to get to Chinese school on time when we're already in Chinatown," Ivy told Julie. "Hey, can you spend the night with me? Gung Gung and Po Po already said it's fine with them."

"I'd love to, but—" Julie glanced at her dad. She was pleased at the invitation, yet she knew her father also wanted to spend time with her. "Is it okay with you, Dad?"

Mr. Albright agreed to the overnight, but he asked Julie to come straight home when Ivy went to her Chinese class in the morning.

"Thanks, Dad!" Julie grinned at Ivy.

Julie and her dad went back out to the car and brought in Julie's overnight bag. Gung Gung, Ivy's grandfather, reached for the bag. "I'll take this upstairs and put it with Ivy's," he said. Julie smiled at the sight of Yue Yan's head poking out from the side pocket.

"Hello, Ivy," said a woman at the birthday party table next to theirs.

"Hello, Mrs. Chan," said Ivy. She introduced Julie to the teacher who gave lessons in reading and writing Chinese. Mrs. Chan introduced Julie to her son, Paul, and two of Paul's friends, Lonny Wu and Mike Gee.

As the girls found seats at their own table, Ivy whispered to Julie that she knew all the boys from the Chinese school. "They're pretty nice," she said, "but that Lonny Wu—the one in the green sweater—is always clowning around. He's the smartest boy in Chinese school, but he's so annoying. He just turned fourteen, and he thinks he knows everything. He's always carrying around his pocket calculator and that backpack full of books!"

Julie rolled her eyes. The boys were jumping up from their chairs, laughing wildly, wielding their chopsticks as swords, pretending to be various superheroes and villains. Sure enough, even while sword fighting with Andrew, Lonny had a calculator sticking out of his shirt pocket. His backpack was slung over the back of his chair.

"I have so much to tell you," Julie murmured to Ivy when she was seated between her friend and Ivy's little sister, Missy. "Bad news first." She told Ivy about the invasion of her bedroom by Olivia Kaminsky. Andrew leaned back in his chair at the party table, listening.

Ivy squeezed Julie's hand. "If it gets too awful, you can move in with us."

"We've got enough girls in the house already," Andrew said. "You'd better stay put."

Julie crossed her eyes at him, but she thought he had a valid point. People *should* stay put. They shouldn't just move in on other people.

The kitchen door kept swinging open and shut as waiters hurried back and forth with trays of tempting foods. When a waiter stopped at their table, Julie ordered green beans with tofu, her favorite. When the appetizers were served—wontons in spicy peanut sauce—Julie was proud that she knew how to use chopsticks almost as well as Ivy, who had taught her years ago when they were both little girls.

When they'd finished their appetizers, and

the adults and Tracy were deep in conversation, Julie pulled the scrap of paper from her pocket and handed it to Ivy. "I found this today," she said. "Can you read it?"

Ivy squinted at the minuscule writing. "It's a strange sort of poem, I think," Ivy said, pointing with her finger from right to left. "*'Bamboo does not grow in our village'*—and it goes on from there, sort of a list... um... hold on. I think I can get it."

She grabbed a pen and a paper take-out menu and started writing the English translation. Julie watched eagerly, marveling at the way her friend could make sense out of the intriguing characters. But when Ivy handed back the page, she looked confused. "I'm not sure I translated it properly," Ivy said. "It's something about a house with four rooms, and some chickens, and a doll... I know, let's ask Lonny Wu. He's always got perfect translations in class."

The girls slid out of their seats and went over to Lonny. The boys were just heading for the buffet table, but Lonny paused when Ivy held out the note. "Can you read this?" she asked, sounding suddenly shy.

Lonny took the note. "What is it?" He read it swiftly and laughed. "Well, if you're planning a future as a poet, you'd better try again. It doesn't make sense!"

"I didn't write it, silly! Look how old it is," said Ivy.

Julie plucked the note out of Lonny's hand. This boy thought he was so cool. "Maybe you're just not translating it correctly," she pointed out.

"Translating what?" inquired Mrs. Chan, on her way back from the buffet table with a plate piled high. She looked with interest at the note Julie held. "Go on and get your plate now, Lonny," Mrs. Chan said to the boy. "The others will be done before you start eating!"

She smiled at the girls as Lonny loped over to the buffet table. "Those boys are gobbling enough food to feed an army, but I hope they save room for dessert." Mrs. Chan winked at Ivy. "I ordered one of your grandmother's special cakes for Paul. And she's putting a whole parade of superheros on top as a surprise."

"My lips are sealed," Ivy promised.

"Well, I hope you'll unseal them to recite in class tomorrow morning," Mrs. Chan teased. "And don't forget that we're having a quiz."

"I'm ready," Ivy said. "As ready as I'll ever be, anyway."

"Oh, I bet she'll ace it," Julie said loyally. "She translated my note in no time at all."

"Well, I must have made some mistakes," said Ivy, "because it really doesn't seem to make sense—just as Lonny said."

"May I see?" Mrs. Chan set her plate down on the table.

"I found it today in an old jacket," Julie explained.

Mrs. Chan looked over the message, eyebrows raised. Then she reached for Ivy's translation. She read it, nodding. "Very well done, Ivy. And you understood that these characters are written in traditional rather than simplified Chinese. I think you'll do just fine on the quiz."

Ivy beamed. Mrs. Chan reached into her

handbag, brought out a pen, and made a few small corrections. "This is very interesting," she said.

Julie read the translation aloud:

— Bamboo does not grow in our village but on hill to the west.
— Uncle Kim's nickname: Big Ears
— House: four rooms, eight windows, separate kitchen. Bedrooms face south.
— From gate to front door seventeen steps. Gate to garden thirty-two steps.
— Eight chickens, one rooster, four geese
— Garden: cabbage, beans, onions, garlic, broccoli
— Mother is housekeeper.
— Father is merchant. Lives in San Francisco. Has four sisters. Visits us every three years.
— Best-loved doll in the world is gift from Father. Keep her very safe on journey, for you cannot sleep without her.
— Grandmother raises rabbits. You make pets of them.

*— Fire burned school last year. School is 100
steps down main lane of village, on left side.
— Keep little duck to bring luck, but give Kai to
Father when you arrive: she will bless you both
with riches until we meet again, my dear Jiao Jie.*

"Hey," exclaimed Ivy, "Jiao Jie is my grandmother's name! Why would she be mentioned
in this list? That's so weird."

Mrs. Chan turned the scrap of paper over,
looking at the tiny characters written on both
sides.

"Well, didn't your grandmother immigrate
to America from China, Ivy?" Mrs. Chan asked.

"Yes. But that was long ago, when she was
just a girl," said Ivy.

"Then I think Julie has found an old coaching note," Mrs. Chan told them.

"What's a coaching note?" Julie asked
Mrs. Chan.

"And who wrote it?" asked Ivy. "And why
so small?"

"I think there's a story here that your

grandmother might like to tell you, Ivy," said the teacher. "In fact, I would dearly like to hear it myself."

"Then let's ask her!" Julie said, pointing. Po Po was just coming through the swinging kitchen door behind two waiters trundling a metal cart laden with food. Steam rose from the silver-lidded bowls. As the waiters set the dishes in the center of their table, Julie's mouth watered. There were platters of vegetables and fish, wafer-thin *mu shu* pancakes to wrap around seasoned meat with savory plum sauce, and fragrant fried rice.

Ivy's grandmother and grandfather stopped at the Chans' table to wish Paul a happy birthday.

"Over here," Ivy beckoned them. "We have something to show you!"

3
JIAO JIE'S JOURNEY

While everyone helped themselves to the food, Julie explained again how she'd found the note in the quilted red jacket. Po Po perched her reading glasses on her nose. Then she and Gung Gung sat at the table, gray heads bent together, reading the note.

Gung Gung's bushy eyebrows rose in puzzlement. But Po Po smiled tremulously. "Amazing. Astonishing!" she said softly. "To think that this note was in the jacket—all these years..."

"You mean it's yours?" asked Ivy.

"Yes indeed. My father must have packed the coat away after it got too small for me. When I was cleaning out old clothes from the cedar chest, the coat must have been with them."

Gung Gung placed his big, work-worn hand

over Po Po's small one. "And the note?"

"I don't even know where to start!" Po Po shook her head. "I suppose I have to go back to when I was a girl just a bit older than Ivy and Julie, back in China."

Mrs. Chan hitched her chair over from the next table and leaned forward eagerly. Her husband pulled his chair over so that he, too, could hear. Po Po's voice drew other listeners from tables nearby. Andrew had been joking around with his friends, but now even the boys pressed close to listen to Po Po's story.

"Back in China in 1919," Po Po told them, "I lived with my mother in our small village. I was fourteen, almost fifteen. My father had written to her that it was time for us to join him in San Francisco. He had been living all alone, working hard to earn money for our family. Now, at last, he was ready for us to come!" Po Po shook her head, tendrils of wispy gray hair falling from her bun. "He wanted us to sail to him on a big ship. But he did not know that my mother was very ill. She had a terrible cough and her lungs were weak. The doctor warned her not to travel, so she decided to send me first and come later herself when she was better. 'Alone?' I said. 'All that way?' But my mother nodded. I was nearly grown, she said. And my father wanted us with him. It was on a cool spring morning when my mother hugged me good-bye."

Po Po had a faraway look in her eyes. "At the dock, my mother tucked the note into my pocket and then kissed my cheek." Po Po's eyes misted, and she took a shaky breath. "Again and again, she reminded me to read the note, to memorize everything on it so that I would be able to pass my interview. 'Memorize every last word!' my mother urged. 'Do you promise?'"

"What interview?" asked Julie.

A tall, thin young man with a long ponytail and a wispy beard spoke up. "Interviews were the usual thing for Chinese immigrants who arrived on Angel Island," he explained.

Julie turned to Ivy. "Who's he?" she mouthed, but Ivy just shrugged.

"The immigrants were quizzed over and

over by the authorities once they arrived at the Immigration Station on Angel Island," the young man continued. "The immigrants were kept on the island while the officials decided whether or not to let them enter. They tested people on all sorts of details about their lives, to make sure they were who they claimed to be."

"You seem well informed," said Gung Gung.

The young man smiled. "My grandparents were stuck on Angel Island for months, waiting to be interviewed. I've heard their stories."

"It was that way for me, too," murmured an old man at the next table.

"Mr. Sing Chen from the Lotus Dry Cleaners," Ivy whispered to Julie.

Po Po's voice trembled a bit. "Imagine this note turning up after so many years!" Continuing her story, she said that she had promised her mother she would study the note every day of the journey. She had promised she would keep it safe and memorize every word. "But that's not what happened," said Po Po. "I know my mother put the note safely into my pocket, but later, when I looked for it, I could not find it!" She shrugged. "I believed I had lost it—perhaps when I pulled out my mittens—and it had somehow blown overboard. Such cold winds were gusting every day that we sailed."

"But instead of blowing overboard, the note must have slipped down into the lining of the red jacket through a tear in the seam," said Julie. "Just think, it's been there all this time!"

Po Po lifted the note to her lips and gave it a kiss. "How wonderful to have something in my own mother's handwriting. You see, I never saw her again. She died soon after I sailed."

Julie could only imagine how terrible that would be. It had been hard enough moving away from her dad after the divorce. But at least he wasn't dead, and she saw him often.

Gung Gung patted Po Po on the back. "There now," he said in his deep, rumbly voice. "It was a long time ago."

"Yes, but how I will treasure this little list. Thank you for finding it, Julie dear."

"Let's hear what it says," said Tracy.

Po Po unfolded the note and read it aloud. Near the end she broke off, shaking her head with a little laugh. "But—my goodness! What an odd thing to write. That was never true."

"What was never true, Po Po?" asked Ivy.

"My mother wrote here that my doll was my best-loved toy, and that I could not sleep without her. But that's a very strange thing for her to write, and she must have known it wasn't true! Kai was just a doll that a neighbor woman gave me a few days before I sailed. I was nearly fifteen, and I no longer played with dolls, but my mother insisted I take it along on the journey. It wasn't anything I cared about at all."

"Really?" said the young man with the ponytail, squinting at the note. He leaned over Ivy's chair as if he wanted to snatch the little paper from Po Po's hand and read it himself.

Mrs. Chan hitched her chair closer to their table. "Probably your mother was confused because she was ill. I'm sure she just thought the doll would be a comfort to you on such a harrowing journey. I loved my dolls as a child—

still collect them today, in fact! I always carried a special one for luck. Perhaps your mother thought the doll she sent with you would bring you luck on your journey."

"My favorite doll is *my* good-luck charm," Ivy spoke up. Ivy's doll, Li Ming, was so well loved, she was beginning to look a little worn, but Ivy still cherished her. The Christmas before last, Ivy had given Julie a doll that was a near twin to Li Ming. Julie had named her doll Yue Yan, and the girls often played together with their dolls. Yue Yan meant "happy and beautiful," and Julie thought it was a perfect name for her beloved doll.

"I suppose my mother might have thought the doll would comfort me," Po Po agreed. She described saying good-bye to her mother, a cold salty wind blowing their parting words away. She boarded the ship and soon met up with a sad girl named Mei Meng, whose parents had died of influenza. Mei was on her way to San Francisco all alone to join her new guardians, a kind man and his wife who had immigrated some years earlier to the "Gold Mountain."

"That's what the Chinese called California," Gung Gung interjected. "Because of the color of the hills in summer, and also because so many believed this was the land of opportunity, where even the streets were paved with gold."

The young man behind Ivy's chair snorted. Julie wished he'd go back to his own table.

"It must have been a terrible disappointment," Mr. Albright said soberly, "when they arrived to find just regular pavement."

"And poverty," said Gung Gung. "But still, for many Chinese, life was better here than in the villages at home."

"Well," continued Po Po, "my new friend Mei came from one of those very poor villages. She was happy to have new guardians in America rather than try to make her way as an orphan in China. But Mei had to pretend that these friends were her parents; otherwise the immigration officials would not allow her into the country. That was the law—only family members of American citizens could immigrate to the United States. Mei was very frightened that she wouldn't pass her interview. But she had been given coaching notes to study that told all about the couple she would be joining, so that the immigration authorities would believe she was their child."

"A paper daughter," said the tall young man with the ponytail. "That's what they called the children who had to pretend they were joining their parents in America. They were paper sons and paper daughters, because they were only sons and daughters on paper—on their travel documents, not in reality."

"What were they in reality?" asked Julie, confused.

"Orphans, like Mei Meng, or sometimes just acquaintances or distant relations who were hoping to find a better life in America," said the young man.

Nodding, Po Po stared across the restaurant, but Julie had the feeling Ivy's grandmother wasn't seeing busy waiters and families dining on all the good food, was no longer smelling the garlic and ginger in the air. Instead, Po Po seemed to be seeing the swells of the ocean waves and smelling salt spray.

In a dreamy voice, Po Po continued her story. Mei studied her coaching notes for hours every day. Jiao Jie—Po Po—spent a lot of time quizzing Mei, until Mei knew all the answers. But Jiao Jie could not find her own coaching note! Still, she was not especially worried, because she was not a paper daughter like Mei, but the true daughter of her father. Surely she knew enough details about her home in China and about her parents and neighbors to convince the officials.

On their last day at sea, the day before their ship was to arrive, the girls threw Mei's coaching notes into the sea. They stood on deck together, listening to the gulls screech and watching the land grow closer and closer. Mei reached for Jiao Jie's hand and squeezed hard.

They transferred from the large ship to a smaller boat that took them to the Immigration Station on Angel Island, in the middle of San Francisco Bay. Jiao Jie's heart beat faster as she lined up with all the other passengers to be marched off the boat and into the building that would be her new home until she could join her father.

If she passed her interview. If she did not, she would be sent back to China and a life of poverty.

The girls were shown to the barracks. Their dormitory was a crowded room lined with metal bunk beds, three tiers high. Women and children sat on the beds or huddled together by the windows, playing cards and talking. The room was warm from all the bodies—too warm, Jiao Jie felt. She longed to throw open those locked windows to let in the fresh air. The voices of all the people hummed around her.

Jiao Jie climbed up into one of the top bunks and hoped she would not fall out in the night. She was glad Mei Meng was sleeping just below her. The bottom bunk held an elderly woman whose loud snores woke Jiao Jie throughout the night. In the morning, Jiao Jie and Mei followed the others to the dining hall, where they sat close together on a wooden bench. Jiao Jie looked with distaste at the thin grayish soup in her bowl and the small portion of unseasoned rice. "Eat it all," said a young woman across from them, her expression bleak. "It's all we get till dinner."

The girls stayed on Angel Island for nearly a month, waiting... waiting. They played with the doll Jiao Jie's mother had given her, and with the little wooden duck Jiao Jie always carried in her pocket for luck. Finally the morning arrived when Jiao Jie was called for her interview.

A young woman interrupted the girls' meager breakfast of oatmeal in the drafty dining hall. The woman was also Chinese. She murmured only, "Time for interview," and led Jiao Jie to a small office. There was a wooden table with a single chair on one side and three chairs on the other side. Three uniformed men sat in those chairs. The woman announced Jiao Jie and then left the room. Jiao Jie twisted her hands together nervously.

One man said something in English that

Jiao Jie could not understand. Another man translated: "Sit, child," he ordered her in Chinese.

Jiao Jie sat, and the questions began. It was not really an interview but an interrogation. She was asked to describe her parents, grandparents, siblings. "I have no siblings," she whispered. Was it a trick question?

The questions continued. In which villages were her parents born? They asked about her house and her school, and the arrangement of buildings in the neighborhood. Were there many trees? What kinds? How far was the school from her home? Describe the teacher. Did she wear a school uniform? Describe her mother's best dress. How many buttons? Homemade or store-bought?

How Jiao Jie wished she had not lost the coaching note her mother had written for her! But she answered carefully, honestly, to the best of her ability. The translator listened and repeated what she told him, turning her words into English words—the same English she would have to learn to find her way in this new country.

But would she be allowed to stay? Would they believe that all the details she told them were true? They *were* true, every one of them, and yet Jiao Jie felt that the men suspected she was lying. Would they ever let her go?

Photographs, each mounted on stiff cardboard, were spread on the table, and Jiao Jie was asked to pick out the picture of her father. At least that was easy. Jiao Jie felt the prick of tears behind her eyes at the familiar face. A copy of this same photograph had stood on her mother's table back home. Jiao Jie picked up the photo and pressed it to her heart. Her hands were shaking. Then she handed it to one of the men.

After what seemed an eternity, the men stood up from the table. They nodded at Jiao Jie and sent her back to the women's dormitory. A full week went by before they summoned her again. This time they smiled. They reached out to shake her hand—an unfamiliar gesture to a girl who bowed as a sign of respect. "Welcome to America," they said. It was the first English Jiao Jie understood.

She had passed the interview! Warm relief flooded through her. She was safe. She would soon be with her father.

"I was overjoyed," Po Po said, looking around at her audience. "I was so eager to leave Angel Island."

Julie breathed a sigh of relief—although she had to laugh a little at herself because obviously Jiao Jie had passed the interview. Here was Po Po, telling them her story, after all.

But then a shadow darkened Po Po's eyes. "I couldn't wait to leave the island—but at the same time, it was so very hard to say good-bye to Mei. She'd been like a sister to me during the hardest time of my life..."

Julie's stomach clenched, remembering how hard it had been to say good-bye to Ivy when they'd moved away from Dad's house and how lonely she'd felt starting a new school without Ivy at her side. She and Ivy were sisters to each other just the way Po Po and her friend Mei had been.

"What happened to Mei?" asked Ivy. "Did she pass her interview?"

"I was so worried for her," Po Po replied. "My own interview had been grueling—and I was telling the truth. How would it be for poor Mei, trying to remember the details she'd memorized of a family that wasn't really her own? And of course the family would need to give the same details in their interview. She was a paper daughter, not a real daughter, and that was a dangerous thing to be in those days." Po Po sat silently for a long moment, and then continued. "I left the island first, before she was interviewed. How we both cried, saying good-bye. I did hear, years later, from one of the women who had shared our dormitory and later settled in San Francisco near us, that Mei passed her interview the very next month and moved with her new parents to Oakland, across the bay."

"Well, that's a happy ending to the story, then," said Julie's dad.

"And did you recognize your father when you saw him?" Julie asked eagerly.

"Oh, yes," said Po Po softly. "He looked just like the photograph he had sent us. And he was very glad to see me—though very sad as well, because while I waited on Angel Island, he received a letter written by our neighbor, saying that my mother had died of her illness." She paused for a moment, lost in thought. Then she smiled. "I remember when my father came to Angel Island to bring me home. It was wonderful to see him, but strange, too; because we had been apart for so many years, I did not know him well. And after the little boat took us to San Francisco, we walked home through the streets of the city. All the sights and sounds and smells—so different from our small village! When we arrived at my new home above my father's produce shop, it felt like a palace to me, though it had only two rooms. But there was running water! At home in China we had to walk to the well."

"No running water?" interrupted Lonny Wu.

"Po Po, that must have been rough!" said Andrew.

"It was what we were used to," said Po Po. "It was all I knew." The boys crowded close to Po Po, listening as she continued.

"As soon as we entered my father's apartment, he asked me to give him what my mother had sent with me. I thought he meant the woolen shawl, and I handed it to him. But Father shook his head. In a low voice he told me he'd asked my mother to bring a special jade necklace when we came to America. It was very valuable and had been in his family for many generations. He had given it to my mother when they married, but now he wanted to sell it, he said, because it would bring a good price, and he needed the money. Life in the Gold Mountain was not nearly as full of riches as he'd hoped. I was so sorry to tell him my mother had not given me a necklace to bring to him. Probably she had planned to bring it herself later, when she'd recovered from her sickness."

"But your mother died," Julie murmured, her heart heavy at the thought. Poor Jiao Jie.

"That's right," continued Po Po, "and we

never did get that necklace, and my father never did make a fortune. But somehow things turned out all right. The shop made my father a good enough living. And he married again after another couple years and had two more children, born right here in San Francisco. The rest of my childhood was happy, though I always did miss my mother." Po Po pressed the note to her cheek. "You have brought me a very special present, Julie dear," she said. "A letter from my mother!"

Julie glowed with pleasure. The people who had been listening smiled, and Julie noticed that even Mrs. Chan had tears in her eyes.

Then two waiters wheeled a cart with a large birthday cake, candles aflame, over to the Chans' table. Everyone turned from Po Po to Paul Chan, who blew out all twelve candles with a single breath. People all around the restaurant clapped and sang "Happy Birthday."

"Speech, speech!" shouted Lonny Wu.

Mrs. Chan shushed him, and then she and Mr. Chan bowed to Po Po for baking such a magnificent cake.

Po Po blushed. "Just don't eat the plastic superheroes," she said, eyes twinkling.

A little girl ran over to the party table, black braids swinging. "How old are you?" she asked Paul. She held up her hand, fingers splayed. "I'm five."

"I'm twelve," said Paul. He looked at his friends and rolled his eyes.

"You have a lot of presents!" The little girl reached out a hand to stroke a package wrapped in silver paper. "I think you have too many!"

"Well, I think I have just the right number." Paul craned his neck. "Don't you have parents?"

"I wanna sit with *you*," the child said.

The boys hooted with laughter. "Scram, kid," said Lonny.

"*I* want a present!" yelled the little girl.

In a flash, a woman swooped down and snatched the girl's hand. "Carrie! Come back and finish your supper."

Carrie pulled her hand away and stamped her foot. "I want a new toy *right now!*"

"We don't have money for new toys."

Julie watched in fascination as the young mother picked Carrie up and took her back to a booth in the far corner of the large room. The little girl kicked and fussed the whole way, drawing stares from the other patrons.

As if the child's behavior had unleashed the birthday party boys' own high spirits, the boys jumped up and started playing a crazy game of catch with their superhero figures. Julie watched as Paul tossed Batman across the table and Andrew deftly caught the toy in midair.

Beyond their table, at a nearby booth, Julie saw a dark head duck out of sight behind the padded seat back. *There's that little girl again!* she thought. Or maybe it was one of the boys, who seemed to have pent-up energy after listening to Po Po's long story. But what a satisfying story it was, Julie thought, and how lucky she felt to have played a small part in it by bringing the old coaching note back into the light of day.

4
VANISHED!

"I think it's time to head home," Julie's dad said. He and Tracy pushed back their chairs and thanked Ivy's grandparents.

"We hope you'll be back to celebrate the Chinese New Year with us at the end of the month," Gung Gung urged.

After all the diners had left, the girls helped clear the tables. Ivy took dishes to the kitchen, and Julie wiped the glass-covered tabletops clean. On the table where the Chans had been sitting, one large piece of birthday cake sat untouched, topped with a plastic Green Hornet figurine. "That cake looks too luscious to throw away!" Julie said as Ivy reached for the plate.

"I know," said Ivy. "And I think I hear my stomach rumbling—even after our big dinner."

"Me too!" Julie grinned. "It would be such a shame to waste it."

Both girls giggled. They plucked the Green Hornet off the frosting and gobbled the last piece of Paul Chan's cake. It was a heavenly confection of rich, dense pound cake layered with jam and topped with fluffy buttercream frosting and ribbons of chocolate. "Mmmm," sighed Julie. "I can sum up this whole evening in one word: Yum."

A waitress passing by with a pile of clean, folded napkins winked.

The girls said good night to the cook and headed upstairs with Gung Gung and Po Po.

"A busy night," said Po Po with a sigh.

Gung Gung opened the apartment door. "And that's what we want, my dear." He ushered his wife and the girls into the apartment. "The busier the better, in the restaurant business."

Julie stepped into the dark living room. The garlic and ginger smells from the restaurant did not rise up to the apartment; instead there was the light, spicy fragrance of the sandalwood incense Po Po liked to burn for luck.

Po Po reached over to switch on a table lamp by the door. Then she let out a gasp. "Something's not right," she whispered.

Gung Gung stepped into the room beside her and looked around. He muttered something in Chinese.

Julie froze, holding her breath. What was wrong? At first glance, nothing seemed amiss. Then she saw.

Po Po was an immaculate housekeeper, yet now the door of the front closet stood open, and one of Gung Gung's hats had tumbled to the floor. On the bookshelf, a small vase lay on its side. In the kitchen, cupboard doors swung gently. Looking toward the two bedrooms, Julie saw that they had also been disturbed. Closet doors stood ajar, and dresser drawers had been pulled open and not completely closed again.

"Someone has been here!" cried Po Po, holding her hands to her mouth.

Gung Gung strode to his desk in the corner. He seized the telephone. "I'm calling the police," he said in a low voice. "Please go back out into the hallway until I search the apartment. Whoever did this might still be here—hiding."

Ivy gasped, and Po Po looked alarmed. They hurriedly stepped back out of the apartment and stood in the hallway, near the door that led to the street. But Julie lingered, not wanting Gung Gung to be left alone.

Gung Gung spoke to the police, reporting what had happened. Then he hung up, nodding at Julie. "They're on their way." He raised his voice. "The police are on their way!" That loud announcement, Julie knew, was for the benefit of anyone under a bed or in a closet. She shivered, watching as Gung Gung went through the apartment, pulling back the floor-length curtains, checking behind the corner armchairs.

Julie followed Gung Gung. He peered in the closets and pulled back the shower curtain. Holding her breath, the hairs at the back of her neck prickling, Julie watched him bend down to look under the beds.

No one.

"All clear," Gung Gung called to Po Po and Ivy.

The police arrived. Po Po closed the door firmly and slid the bolt. "Put on water for tea, girls," she said, "while we talk to the officers."

In the small kitchen, Ivy turned on the fire under the tea kettle. While waiting for the water to boil, she and Julie left the kitchen and went into the guest bedroom. Ivy looked at the open closet door. "I don't like knowing someone was in here, touching things," she said uneasily.

"It's creepy," Julie agreed. She lingered in the doorway between the guest bedroom and the living room, watching the police search the apartment.

The officers asked Gung Gung and Po Po what was missing. "Money? Jewelry?"

Po Po shook her head. "I just checked the bedroom, and my jewelry box is still there, unopened."

"That's the funny thing," said Gung Gung. "Nothing seems to be missing at all."

Just then Ivy pushed past Julie and burst into

the living room. "Wait—something *is* missing!" she cried out. "*Li Ming* is missing!"

Po Po and Gung Gung hurried to the bedroom. The police officers looked concerned. "Who is Li Ming?" they asked, following Ivy's grandparents. They looked relieved when Ivy explained that Li Ming was her doll.

Julie ran back into the bedroom. She stared at the empty side pocket of her suitcase. Gung Gung had brought the overnight bags upstairs, and Yue Yan had been in the side pocket. Julie remembered how the doll's head had stuck out comically.

The police duly noted a description of the missing dolls. "Are your dolls valuable?" they asked the girls.

Li Ming and Yue Yan were nearly identical Chinese dolls. They were well made, with smooth plastic bodies and soft, shiny black hair. But Julie doubted they had been particularly expensive.

"Li Ming's valuable to me!" said Ivy, and the officers smiled.

"Yue Yan is valuable to me, too," Julie told the officers. "Ivy gave her to me. She's special." But she suspected they would not look very hard for either doll.

As the girls helped tidy up the apartment, Julie tried to picture what had happened while they were downstairs in the restaurant. An intruder had sneaked upstairs and searched the apartment. Someone had taken her doll from her overnight bag, and Ivy's doll, too. The dolls were each only about a foot tall and could have been hidden inside someone's jacket or a large purse. Someone had found them and taken them away...

But why? Who would want two dolls?

Then she recalled, with a stab of unease, the little girl who had fussed in the restaurant because she wanted a present. Could she have slipped upstairs unseen and taken some presents for herself?

5
A Troubling Discovery

As the girls got ready for bed, Julie told Ivy her suspicion. "Ivy, remember that girl who wanted a toy so badly?"

Ivy nodded. "Carrie, her name was."

"Yes," Julie said. "Carrie. Maybe when her mom wasn't paying attention, she ran up here and stole Li Ming and Yue Yan."

"Gung Gung doesn't usually lock the apartment door when he's down in the restaurant," Ivy said thoughtfully. "And that girl kept running away from her table. She could have just let herself in when her mom wasn't looking! Let's ask if my grandparents know them."

When the girls asked, Po Po nodded. "I met them tonight, when the young mother applied for the bookkeeping job."

"So you have their phone number?"

"Yes, but why?" Ivy's grandmother raised her eyebrows as Ivy explained. "Well," Po Po said, "I doubt such a young child could reach the cupboards—and whoever came in here opened every cupboard door in the apartment. Still, I suppose it's possible. It's too late to phone anyone now, so we'll wait till tomorrow. If that wild child has your dolls, they'll be safe enough for the night."

❖

Julie lay in the bed next to Ivy's in Po Po and Gung Gung's guest room. Her body ached with tiredness, but her mind still whirled with the events of the day. Discovering the note in the red jacket... Learning she'd be losing her bedroom... Hearing Po Po's story over dinner... Coming upstairs to find the apartment ransacked and the much-loved dolls stolen...

A line from the coaching note popped into Julie's head: *Best-loved doll in the world is gift from*

A Troubling Discovery

Father. Keep her very safe on journey, for you cannot sleep without her.

Maybe Jiao Jie hadn't needed her doll to sleep well, but Julie felt strange without Yue Yan at her side. And poor Ivy tossed restlessly without Li Ming. It took Julie a long time to fall asleep.

On Saturday morning, the girls packed up their overnight things. As Julie zipped her bag closed, she remembered again how Yue Yan's pretty little head had peeked out. From Ivy's sad expression, Julie knew her friend was thinking about her missing doll, too.

Po Po promised to phone Carrie's mother while Ivy was at Chinese school. She and Gung Gung hugged the girls at the kitchen door.

Po Po indicated a plastic trash bag at the side of the kitchen door. "Would you girls mind taking that to the alley on your way out?"

Julie hefted the bag. "No problem!"

The alley behind the restaurant was narrow and full of metal cans piled high with boxes and bags. Some of the bags had been ripped open, perhaps by stray dogs. Vegetable scraps spilled out of a torn bag. And—*Wait.* Julie squinted. Something else was there, partially hidden beneath the decaying vegetables: Feet. Exceedingly small ones. *Doll-sized* feet.

Julie dropped the trash bag she was holding and plunged her hand into the garbage. And there was Li Ming—or at least part of Li Ming. The little doll's body, still in its lovely red dress, was covered in onion skins and limp cabbage leaves. And there, right on the ground by the metal can, was Li Ming's plastic head, popped right off the neck.

Ivy cried out and dropped to her knees, reaching for the pieces of her doll. "Why?" she asked. "Why would someone do this?"

Hastily, Julie started opening other bags of garbage, searching for Yue Yan.

"Li Ming is the best doll!" Tears streamed down Ivy's face, but her mouth was tight and angry as she tried to fit the head back onto the doll's body. "Julie, if Carrie did this, we need to tell the police!" Impatiently Ivy dashed away her tears. "Don't worry," she crooned to the doll.

"We'll fix you up good as new—and after that I promise to keep you safe."

With Ivy's words echoing in her head, Julie pulled her arms out of the last garbage bag. She wiped her hands on her jeans and dug into her back pocket for the coaching note translation. She unfolded it and read it again.

Best-loved doll in the world . . . Keep her very safe. And then: *. . . give Kai to Father . . . she will bless you both with riches until we meet again.*

An idea stirred in the back of Julie's mind, but she couldn't pin it down. Something about dolls . . . something about Po Po's doll? But how could Po Po's doll be connected to Li Ming and Yue Yan?

And where was Yue Yan?

6
WRITTEN IN CODE?

The girls ran inside with Ivy's doll. They found Po Po in the dining room, arranging little bouquets for the restaurant tables. "Why, girls! What brings you back? Ivy, you'll be late for your class, and Mrs. Chan will not be pleased."

"Julie found my doll," Ivy cried. "But look at her!"

"Oh my!" Po Po examined Li Ming carefully as the girls washed up. "What in the world?" She inspected the doll's plastic neck. "Well, I think I can fix this," she said. "You go on to your class, Ivy dear. I'll put Li Ming back together and clean her up while you're gone."

Ivy wrapped Po Po in a hug. "Thanks!"

"It's hard to understand who would do a thing like this." Po Po looked puzzled. "And what about your doll, Julie?"

"We couldn't find her," Julie said.

Po Po glanced at her watch. "It's a mystery why anyone would break in and take your dolls," she said. "But an even bigger mystery right now is how Ivy is going to explain to Mrs. Chan that she's late for class even though you both spent the night right here in Chinatown! Hurry along now, and I'll fix Li Ming while you're gone."

Julie headed back to her dad's house, deep in thought. The morning was misty, but as she looked out over San Francisco Bay from the top of a steep street, she saw that the fog was lifting. She could see Alcatraz Island, where the old prison was, and the larger island—Angel Island—where young Jiao Jie and her friend Mei had been detained at the Immigration Station so many years ago. Now both islands were open to visitors. Tracy had gone to both last year on a school field trip, Julie recalled.

Julie started walking down the hilly street. She thought about the interviews Po Po and Mei had been subjected to. How many steps from their houses to their schools? What a strange question! Julie tried to figure out the number of steps from her apartment to her own school. Hundreds! What if she were ever required to answer such weird questions? She would surely need a coaching note like the ones written out for young Jiao Jie and Mei.

It was sad that the girls had never seen each other again, Julie thought. She would hate to lose touch with Ivy.

Rounding the corner, Julie counted the steps up the walk to her dad's house. She pulled the translation of the coaching note from her pocket and sat on the front steps to read the part about the doll again.

Best-loved doll in the world is gift from Father. Keep her very safe on journey, for you cannot sleep without her.

Keep little duck to bring luck, but give Kai to Father when you arrive: she will bless you both with riches until we meet again...

It was very sad that Jiao Jie and her mother never did meet again. But why, Julie wondered, would Jiao Jie's mother write that Kai was a doll Jiao Jie could not sleep without, when she knew perfectly well that Jiao Jie had only just been given the doll?

Even if the mother was very ill, it was a strange mistake.

An idea was forming in the back of Julie's mind, as nebulous as the fog that lay on the waters of San Francisco Bay.

Julie could hear Dad and Tracy laughing in the kitchen. She called hello to them and then went up to her room and lay on her bed. She loved her bedroom in Dad's house. Here was the soft shag rug and the pretty flowered wallpaper she'd picked out back in second grade. Her room at Mom's was bright and full of trendy stuff she'd chosen from Gladrags; it was funny how the two rooms could be so different, yet both reflect parts of her.

Julie wished she had Nutmeg to cuddle, but her pet now lived at Ivy's house. Thorny problems always seemed to untangle themselves when her arms were wrapped around the rabbit's silky warmth. Nutmeg made her feel cozy and safe...

Keep her very safe on journey... you cannot sleep without her... she will bless you both with riches...

Julie remembered the police asking if Li Ming and Yue Yan were valuable. Julie was pretty sure they weren't—but perhaps the thief had believed they were...

Julie glanced at the note. Was *Kai* valuable?

The telephone rang, and after a moment Tracy called up the stairs, "Julie! It's Ivy's grandmother on the phone for you."

Julie went to her dad's bedroom and picked up the extension on his bedside table. "Hello?" she said politely.

"Julie dear," began Po Po, "I just wanted to tell you that Carrie's mother stopped by the restaurant after you left. Gung Gung and I offered her the job as our new bookkeeper. I told her about our intruder, and she was appalled. Carrie was there, too, and she seemed truly shocked that your dolls were stolen. I really don't think that child is our intruder."

WRITTEN IN CODE?

"No, I don't think Carrie did it, either," said Julie. "I don't think a kid who wants new toys would pull off Li Ming's head and throw her in the garbage! It wouldn't make sense." Julie hesitated. She knew there was no reason to think Po Po's doll was connected to Li Ming and Yue Yan, but she couldn't shake the feeling that the coaching note had something to do with the dolls' theft. "Po Po? Was—was Kai valuable?"

"Kai? No, not at all."

"But the coaching note said—"

Po Po's voice chuckled through the phone line. "Kai was just a rag doll, made by a woman in my village. I didn't even play with dolls anymore, so I gave it away to Mei the day I was leaving Angel Island. Mei liked Kai and, goodness knows, she needed something to comfort her while she waited to be interviewed."

"That was kind of you," Julie said. "It's sad that you've never seen Mei since then."

"I had a Christmas card from her once," Po Po said, sounding wistful. "But that was all. I'm sorry we lost touch." Her voice grew brisk.

"Anyway, I just wanted to let you know that I think little Carrie is in the clear."

Julie thanked her for calling and hung up. She sat back on her dad's bed, thinking things over. Dolls, dolls, and more dolls. Yue Yan, who was missing. Li Ming, who had been thrown in the trash. Kai, who was just a rag doll, not special or valuable at all.

But then why had Po Po's mother written that the doll would bring riches?

❖

After lunch, when she knew Ivy would be home from Chinese school, Julie crossed the street and knocked on the Lings' door.

Ivy's little sister, Missy, opened the door. "Po Po reattached Li Ming's head," she reported.

"I'm glad," said Julie, smiling at Missy. She went upstairs and found Ivy playing with Nutmeg. "Your grandmother called me to say that Carrie isn't our thief."

"She called me, too," said Ivy. "So we'll have

to work harder to track down who took Yue Yan. We've got to find her."

"I know," said Julie. "I've been trying to figure out why anyone would want the dolls, and all I can think is that someone believed they were valuable. Then the thief decided Li Ming wasn't and threw her away."

"But why should Yue Yan be valuable and not Li Ming?" Ivy looked skeptical. "They're the same kind of doll!"

Julie shrugged. She didn't understand it, either. But the fact was that Yue Yan was still missing. And something else kept bothering her. She explained it to Ivy: "I think it's weird that we were just talking about dolls last night at dinner, when your grandmother was reading about Kai, and then our dolls disappeared. It seems like too much of a coincidence."

"But how could they be connected?" asked Ivy. "It doesn't make sense."

"I know. But just in case, let's make a list of all the people who listened to Po Po's story at the restaurant last night," Julie said. "Maybe somebody heard Po Po talk about her doll and then got the idea to steal *our* dolls."

"I still can't see why anyone would want our dolls," said Ivy. "Except for Carrie."

Julie chewed her lip, thinking. "Maybe it's somehow connected to what Po Po's mother wrote in the coaching note."

"What do you mean?"

"I keep thinking that it's just so weird what Po Po's mom wrote about Kai. Why would she write something she knew wasn't true?" Julie lay back on Ivy's bed.

"She made a mistake," said Ivy, "because she was so sick."

But what if that wasn't it at all? Julie wondered. *What if Po Po's mother had known exactly what she was writing?*

Abruptly Julie sat up. She felt as if the fog in her brain had cleared. "Ivy! What if Po Po's mother was writing in code?"

Ivy's eyes widened. "Julie's flipped," she whispered into Nutmeg's long ear.

"Maybe . . ." said Julie slowly. "But . . . remember

'the walnuts in the fridge'?"

When Julie and Tracy were little, their mother had read an article about a child kidnapped from school. "The kidnapper wasn't a stranger," Julie remembered her mother fretting. "That's why the child got into the car." So Mom had chosen a code phrase for her daughters to memorize. If ever she or Dad could not pick them up after school and had to send someone else, Mom had explained, that adult would be told the special phrase. If anyone offered them a ride, Julie and Tracy were supposed to listen for the code phrase. If they heard it, they would know that it was safe to accept the ride. But if the driver didn't say the code, the girls were not to get into the car. Mrs. Albright had chosen a code phrase that no kidnapper would guess: "The walnuts are in the fridge."

One day when Julie was in first grade, she had waited on the playground after school, but no one had come to pick her up. Julie was just going inside to tell her teacher when Ivy's mom pulled up. "Hi, Julie," Mrs. Ling called from the car. "Your mom took Tracy to the dentist. You're to come home with me. Hop in, sweetie!"

Julie had grinned at Ivy, Andrew, and baby Missy in the backseat and then narrowed her eyes. "Hmm," she had said, making her voice sound doubtful. "How do I know you aren't secretly a kidnapper?"

Mrs. Ling had smiled. "Good girl!" she said. "Come home with us, and we'll make a snack from *the walnuts in the fridge!*"

And Julie had hopped into the car.

"So by writing something Po Po would know wasn't true, maybe her mother was trying to tell her something," Julie explained to Ivy now. "Something she couldn't write in the note."

"So she said it in code?" asked Ivy dubiously. "Well, what did she mean to say?"

"I don't know. And neither does Po Po."

"So... nobody knows," murmured Ivy.

"Oh yes, someone knows," said Julie quietly, and the hairs on the back of her neck prickled. "The thief figured it out."

7

CHINATOWN CHASE

"All right. Let's make that list." Ivy picked up a pen and a notebook from her desk. "It'll be a long one."

Julie knew it would be. The Happy Panda was one of the most popular restaurants in Chinatown, and there had been plenty of people eating there last night.

"There was Mr. Louie Fong from the bakery," Ivy began, writing his name, "but he's the sweetest man. He'd never steal anything." She crossed off his name. "And there was the dentist and his wife"—two more names written, then immediately crossed off—"and Mr. Yep, the mechanic, but he goes bowling with Gung Gung ... and there were the ladies who play mah-jongg with Po Po, but they're her friends; they'd never sneak into her apartment." She wrote and crossed off several more names. "Oh, and Mr. Sing Chen, who owns the Lotus Dry Cleaners. My grandmother takes Gung Gung's shirts there every week. And the Chans were there, and Paul's friends from the birthday party—Lonny Wu and Mike Gee. And wasn't Mike's dad there, too?" Ivy jotted the names. "Mike wouldn't do something so mean. In Chinese class he likes to make people laugh, only Mrs. Chan gets mad because he always tells her that learning Chinese is a waste of time since we live in America. And he says school on Saturday is downright un-American!"

"It isn't a waste of time learning Chinese," Julie declared. "I wish I could speak another language. And if nobody around here knew Chinese, we couldn't have translated the note!"

"True," said Ivy. "Still, I wish that Chinese school weren't on Saturdays. Mike Gee is right about that, at least."

Firmly, she crossed off Mr. Gee's name, and Mike's, and then all the names on their list. "It just can't be any of these people. Let's forget it."

"I think it was," Julie insisted. "Wait! What about that tall guy with the ponytail?"

"I don't know his name," said Ivy. "But I suppose it could be him. He's the only one I don't know personally, anyway." She wrote "ponytail guy" on her list as their top suspect. Then she capped her pen and closed the notebook. "Listen, *my* doll was in the trash, so maybe yours is too. We should go back to Chinatown and start looking in the alleys before the trash gets picked up on Monday."

"Let's go tomorrow," Julie said.

❖

After dinner, Julie played chess with her dad while Tracy whipped up a batch of brownies for dessert. So far Julie and Dad had won one game apiece and were now on the tie-breaking third. Neatly capturing one of Dad's pawns, Julie said, "Ivy and I would like to go back to Chinatown and look for Yue Yan."

Mr. Albright frowned down at the chessboard. "Where will you look? I don't want you girls getting mixed up in anything dangerous."

"We'll just look in the trash cans," Julie said vaguely. She didn't want to mention that they hoped to track down the thief as well.

He reached out and moved his knight. "Aha!" he exclaimed. "Check."

Julie groaned. "That was sneaky, Dad!" But she saw how he'd done it. He had distracted her with his pawn, all the while moving closer to her king. As she studied the board, looking for a way to escape, she was reminded that they had all been distracted in the restaurant, eating and talking, while a thief had sneaked upstairs.

And that reminded her of Olivia Kaminsky, sneaking into their life and into Julie's bedroom.

Julie quickly moved her queen. "There. Now I'm safe!"

"Hmm." Mr. Albright narrowed his eyes. "Safe for now, maybe..."

"Brownies, anyone?" asked Tracy, coming in with a plateful of warm chocolate.

CHINATOWN CHASE

❁

Sunday morning Julie rode her bike across the street to Ivy's house, carrying with her a stalk of celery for Nutmeg. Ivy and her family were at the breakfast table. Mrs. Ling poured Julie a cup of jasmine tea. "And how about a blueberry muffin?" she asked.

"Thank you," said Julie, taking one.

"While we're looking for Yue Yan," said Ivy, "we should also ask if anyone knows Mei Meng."

"That's a great idea!" Julie said. "Wouldn't it be great if Po Po and Mei could meet up again after so long?"

Ivy's mother smiled. "Po Po would be delighted. I'm sure we'd all like to meet her old friend!"

The girls set off on their bikes, careful on the busy streets to keep close to the curb. Pumping up the steep, hilly streets left Julie breathless, but soaring down the hills felt like flying.

As the girls labored up the last hill, they heard the putt-putt of a motor. Julie glanced over to see a yellow motorbike climbing the hill just behind them. The driver was hunched low over the handlebars, but he turned his helmeted head to nod at the girls as he passed them and crested the hill.

In Chinatown, Ivy led the way. The first place she stopped was Louie's Number One Bakery. "Chinese school is right upstairs," Ivy told Julie. "The smells from all the baking drive me crazy while Mrs. Chan is droning on!"

The display of sun cakes, moon cakes, and sweetheart cakes in the window made Julie hungry again. Inside, the man behind the counter welcomed them heartily. Ivy introduced him to Julie—Mr. Louie Fong, a portly older gentleman whom Julie remembered seeing at the Happy Panda on Friday. The girls asked for a big, flaky sweetheart cake to share.

As Julie and Ivy fished in their pockets for coins to pay for the sugar-dusted pastry, Louie shook his head. "Nothing doing," Louie said to Ivy, handing them each a round, flat sweetheart cake. "Your grandparents have insisted I eat for free at the Happy Panda so many times over so many years! Now you must let me treat you and your friend."

Grinning, the girls thanked him. Then Julie cleared her throat. "So, you've known Ivy's grandparents for a long time?" she began.

"Ah, yes. I was only about twenty when I met your grandfather, Ivy. He was an apprentice chef at the same restaurant where I was a waiter."

"And you met my grandmother then, too?" asked Ivy.

"They were not married yet, back then. But we all became friends," Louie said, nodding. He laughed. "We were each trying to make a living. But it wasn't all work. Such parties we had!"

"Did you ever meet my grandmother's old friend, Mei Meng?" Ivy inquired.

Louie cocked his head. "Hmm. That's the girl from the ship?"

The girls nodded eagerly, but he shook his head. "No, sorry. I didn't know her. Didn't her new family live in Oakland? Why not ask Mrs. Tan over at the Lucky Five and Dime? She moved here from Oakland's Chinatown. It's like a small town over there. Everybody in each other's pockets all the time, knowing everybody's business." He chuckled. "Just like here."

"Thanks," said Julie. "We'll ask her."

The girls thanked him again for the sweetheart cakes and left. They hurried around the corner to check the alley behind the bakery. The bins were full of boxes and packing material from nearby gift shops, but a careful search turned up no sign of Julie's doll. Julie felt guilty even suspecting that nice Mr. Fong might have had anything to do with the dolls' disappearance. Then, just as she was mounting her bike, Julie saw a flash of bright blue on the ground behind a tall stack of wooden crates.

She dropped her bike and ran over. Kneeling down, heart pounding, she reached behind the tower of crates. Her fingers touched soft hair. "Yue Yan!" shouted Julie triumphantly. She drew out her doll, which had been wedged between the rough wooden crates and the back of the building.

"You found her!" Ivy laid her bike on its side and ran over to Julie.

"At least her head's still on," Julie said, trembling a little with relief—and anger as she noticed that the head was turned backward. "Look—Ivy, look! I think the thief took off Yue Yan's head, too, and then popped it back on." She indicated the torn collar of Yue Yan's blue silk dress.

"That's so weird," said Ivy. "But at least you have her back. Thank goodness!"

"Yes," agreed Julie slowly. Tucking the doll under her arm, she picked up her bike and straddled it. She looked around the alley, at the row of closed back doors to souvenir shops and to Louie's Number One Bakery. It was impossible to believe that Mr. Fong had taken the doll. And yet, here was Yue Yan.

Julie shivered as a cold wind whisked down the alley. She looked up at the windows above the bakery, where the Chinese school was held. Could it have been someone from the Chinese school? One of the boys from the party? Or . . .

Puzzle of the Paper Daughter

I loved my dolls as a child—still collect them today, in fact! Julie heard the words in her head again, exactly as Mrs. Chan had spoken them that night in the restaurant.

Could Yue Yan and Li Ming have been stolen by Mrs. Chan herself?

❖

"We've found Yue Yan, but we haven't found Mei Meng," Julie said after she'd kissed Yue Yan and zipped the doll safely inside her jacket. "Let's go to the Lucky Five and Dime, as Mr. Fong suggested."

"You don't really think Mr. Fong stole our dolls, do you?" Ivy asked as they set off on their bikes. "He's such a nice man! I can't believe it."

"I don't know what to think," Julie said tersely. "But—"

The chug of a motorbike drowned out her next words, and there was the same yellow motorbike that had passed them earlier on their way to Chinatown. As the driver rounded the corner, a long ponytail flew out behind his helmet. The driver nodded at the girls. His tinted visor shielded his eyes, but this time Julie could see that he had a soft, wispy beard.

Julie gasped. "That's him!" she yelled to Ivy.

The street became so steep that the girls jumped off their bikes and started walking them up to the top of the hill. "That was definitely the ponytail guy from the restaurant," Julie said, panting slightly.

"Is he following us?"

"I'm not sure," said Julie. Was he the thief? Did he know they had found Yue Yan? Was he following them now, hoping to take the doll again? "All I know is he was there that night, listening to Po Po's story. He heard her reading the part of the note that says Kai 'will bless you both with riches.' That might have made him think one of *our* dolls was Kai and would bless him with riches, or something."

"But Po Po says Kai wasn't valuable," Ivy objected.

"True, but *he* doesn't know that," said Julie.

They were at the top of the hill now. There in front of them was the Lucky Five and Dime—with the yellow motorbike parked outside.

"Is this guy following *us?*" Ivy demanded. "Or are we following him?"

"Well, let's go in," said Julie decisively. "We'll ask what he wants."

Julie pulled open the glass door and stepped inside. A bell jangled to alert the clerk that customers had arrived. Julie glanced around the bustling shop but saw no sign of the young man.

Ivy raised her voice over the constant jangle of the door bell to greet the elderly woman sitting on a stool at the cash register. Ivy spoke first in Chinese and then switched to English. "Excuse me, are you Mrs. Tan?"

"I am," said the old lady in a high, reedy voice. She adjusted her cat-eye glasses and peered at them. "And who are you?"

Ivy introduced herself and Julie and explained that Mr. Fong had said she might know Mei Meng.

"This Mei Meng must be a very popular lady,"

commented Mrs. Tan. She tipped her head toward the front of the store. "He also searches for her."

Julie swung around in time to catch a glimpse of the helmeted motorbike driver slipping out the shop door as the bell jangled.

"Who is that guy?" she demanded.

"I see him at Yep's Garage," said Mrs. Tan. "But why are you looking so unhappy? He is a friend of your friend, this Mei Meng, yes? So that makes him a friend of yours."

"Mei Meng isn't actually our friend," said Julie. "And that guy is definitely not our friend. We don't even know him."

"Mei came from China when she was about fourteen or fifteen," Ivy added. "She and my grandmother met on board the ship, and they were together on Angel Island."

"Hmm," said Mrs. Tan musingly. "I know your grandmother's Happy Panda. Everybody does! Good food! But when I eat out, I prefer going back to Oakland. I lived over there most of my life, you see." She paused to answer a customer's query about an electric rice cooker and then turned her attention back to the girls.

"I prefer Oakland's climate, really," she told them. "Not so much fog! But I moved here two years ago to help my son run this shop."

"Mr. Fong told us that you lived in Oakland for a long time," said Julie. "He thought you might have heard of Mei Meng."

"Well, there was a little girl named Mei-Mei who came to my shop every day to buy white rabbits," Mrs. Tan said. "Would you like one, too?"

Julie blinked, baffled by the question.

Mrs. Tan reached out a wrinkled hand and lifted the lid from a porcelain bowl near the cash register. "Have one. White rabbits are popular with children. And not only children!" She took one in her thin fingers. "I like them myself."

Eagerly Ivy reached for one of the wrapped sweets. "I love these, too."

The old woman popped one into her own mouth. "Little Mei-Mei wouldn't be the one you're seeking, I think. Too young. But there's Mrs. Mei Chung, and Mrs. Mei Liu. But no Mei Meng that I recall." At the girls' disappointed expressions, Mrs. Tan raised one finger. "Here's an idea. You could go around the corner and have a pot of tea at Mr. Long's teahouse. Mr. Long was detained on Angel Island for a time. And he lived in Oakland for many years—ran a teahouse there before opening one here."

The next customer in line was Ivy's teacher, Mrs. Chan, with an armload of notebooks and a box of pencils. The jade green scarf around her neck looked cheerful on the windy, gray day.

"Mrs. Chan—hello!" Ivy said with surprise.

Mrs. Chan did not look at all cheerful. She frowned at the girls as she completed her purchase and then beckoned them to step away from the counter. "I couldn't help but overhear," she said quietly. "Are you girls pestering people about that old coaching note? Does your grandmother know you are playing detective?"

"We're not playing anything," Julie replied, surprised at the Chinese teacher's irritation.

Why should Mrs. Chan be questioning them? What business was it of hers?

"My grandmother would like to see her old friend again," Ivy explained. "It would be nice for them to meet each other again, that's all."

"Well, if you're going to wander around Chinatown asking questions, it would at least be a chance for you to practice speaking Chinese," Mrs. Chan suggested.

"That's a good idea," Ivy replied politely. But Julie felt uneasy.

As the girls left the shop, Julie looked over her shoulder to see Mrs. Chan frowning right back at her. A chill crept across Julie's shoulder blades. Inside her jacket, Yue Yan pressed against Julie's chest reassuringly. *Does Mrs. Chan know I've found Yue Yan?* Julie wondered. *And does she really just want Ivy to practice her Chinese more—or does she object to our asking questions in any language?*

8

TALK IN THE TEAHOUSE

The girls walked their bikes around the corner to Mr. Long's teahouse. Ivy led the way inside, speaking to the waitress in Chinese.

"I told her we wanted to talk to Mr. Long about his time on Angel Island and his teahouse in Oakland," Ivy whispered to Julie.

Julie nodded, wishing she knew Chinese. Next year at school her class would start learning Spanish. At least that would be something.

The waitress answered Ivy in Chinese and then smiled at Julie. "Please have a seat until Mr. Long is free."

The girls sat on the bench by the door and watched the waitress serve customers their tea. In the warm teahouse, Julie's chill subsided. She unzipped her coat and set Yue Yan on the tabletop. Finally Mr. Long, a tall, thin man with a white mustache, came out from the kitchen. He wiped his hands on his apron. "Mrs. Wu tells me you young ladies are asking about Angel Island. You have been there?" Without waiting for their reply, he shook his head. "I was younger than you when I was held there! A whole month—and me, just a little fellow."

"A month!" Ivy's eyes widened.

The door opened and a familiar figure swaggered into the teahouse. It was Lonny Wu, one of the boys from the birthday party. He hugged his skateboard against his green sweater and walked straight over to the waitress.

"Hey, Ma," he said. "I left my key at home."

"Baseball practice over already?" The waitress looked toward the door. "Where are the other boys?"

He shrugged. "Going for ice cream."

His mother's smile was sad. "You want to go, too? Maybe get a single scoop?"

"Nah. We'd better save the money."

"You're a good boy," she said, dipping her

hand into her apron pocket. She withdrew a key ring and slid one key off.

"Thanks, Ma!" Lonny turned to leave and then saw the girls chatting with Mr. Long. He nodded his hello. He looked surprised to see Yue Yan sitting on the table next to Julie. "Taking your baby out for a stroll?" he asked mockingly, one eyebrow raised. "Looks like it needs a bath, if you ask me."

"Just ignore him," whispered Ivy.

Julie shrugged. She was so glad to have Yue Yan back again, she didn't care if Lonny teased her for bringing along a doll.

"Those were dark days," Mr. Long was saying. "My parents had come to Oakland years earlier and started a teahouse like this one. They left me in China with my grandparents and sent for me later. I had travel documents with me, but still the immigration authorities suspected I was not who the documents said I was. They thought I was only a paper son. It took many weeks before I was allowed to leave the island."

"Stories like that make me mad," Lonny said,

his attention diverted from the doll. His voice was resentful. "Angel Island might as well have been Alcatraz—the prison island—for Chinese immigrants. They were treated like dirt."

"Now, Lonny," chided his mother.

"I've been reading about those days. The American dream of opportunity for all—hah!" Lonny continued. "That wasn't a dream the Chinese immigrants were supposed to have. And maybe we're still not," he muttered, looking at his mother. "I think a lot of us are still underpaid and overworked. *If* we've got jobs at all!"

"Lonny!" hissed his mother, with a quick glance at her employer. "Mind your manners. We do all right. Maybe not as well as when your father had steady work, but he'll find something again soon."

"I wish I were sixteen," Lonny grumbled. "Then I'd be old enough to work."

"Your boy is growing up fast," Mr. Long observed to Mrs. Wu. "Soon he is a man. Send him to me when he is sixteen, and I will see if there is a place for him in the teahouse."

Mrs. Wu laughed lightly. "Thank you, I will. But—soon a man, you say? Lonny is just turning fourteen. He is still mostly a boy, Mr. Long. You should see him playing superheroes with his brother!"

Lonny scowled. "So?" Then he turned to Ivy. "That reminds me, does your granny have any more of those thingamajigs from Paul's cake? I lost my Green Hornet."

"His favorite character." His mother beamed. "And his favorite color! I make him a green sweater."

Lonny looked embarrassed. Ivy glanced guiltily at Julie, and Julie shrugged, biting back a smile. That big piece of cake they'd eaten must have been Lonny's. Julie remembered that they'd left the plastic Green Hornet on the table.

"I'll ask my grandmother," Ivy said. Then she turned back to Mr. Long and asked if he'd ever met Mei Meng on Angel Island or when he lived in Oakland.

Lonny leaned against the door, listening. Mr. Long thought for a moment and then shook his head. "The name's not familiar," he said ruefully. "But my old brain is getting forgetful these days. Or," he added with a smile, "could be the lady didn't drink tea and never came to my teahouse!" Mr. Long paused, then added, "You could take the ferry to Angel Island. The park rangers may have old records about people detained there. Maybe you'll find some mention of your grandmother's friend."

"That's a good idea," Julie said. "Have you been there, now that it's a park?"

Mr. Long shook his head. "You won't see me going back. No, sir, I'm not setting foot on that island ever again. Too many ghosts." A faraway look shadowed his eyes. "Locked up inside most of the day and night, some folks carved poetry right into the walls. I wonder if it's still there." He smiled at Ivy. "I hope you find your grandmother's old friend. It's good for those of us who remember what it was like then to get together and talk." He winked. "Talk, and share a pot of hot tea!"

As Julie sailed downhill with the wind in her

face and Yue Yan securely stashed inside her jacket again, she thought of that old man as a little boy shut away on Angel Island. Suddenly she shared Lonny's anger. Mr. Long had been locked up only because he had immigrated from China instead of some other country. The "land of opportunity" had not welcomed the Chinese as it had so many other groups of newcomers.

Then she thought of another newcomer to San Francisco, seeking new opportunities, arriving soon—to their own apartment, for goodness' sake. But that was entirely different, Julie told herself firmly. Olivia Kaminsky wasn't an immigrant; she was an intruder.

The yellow motorbike chug-chugged up the hill past them. "This is too much," Julie said, stopping her bike. She pointed. "Look—he's headed straight for Mr. Long's teahouse! I know he's after something."

Ivy nodded. "You're right. He's going everywhere we are!"

Julie half wanted to return to the teahouse and confront the motorbike driver, demanding to know what he wanted. But if he was up to no good, would he be likely to tell them?

The girls pedaled on to the Happy Panda. By the time they arrived at the restaurant, Julie's and Ivy's cheeks were flushed. They chained their bikes together in the alley and entered through the restaurant's back door.

The kitchen was bustling as Gung Gung and Po Po directed their employees on the day's specials. As Ivy gave her grandmother a hug, Julie unzipped her jacket and withdrew Yue Yan triumphantly.

"You've found the kidnapped child!" Po Po exclaimed. "Well, this calls for celebration. Come and tell me all about it. Oh, such red cheeks you have!" Then Po Po paused, and her voice became softer. "I remember that my friend Mei had rosy cheeks," she said. She smiled at the girls. "That coaching note seems to have unlocked a lot of memories. I've been thinking about my old friend all day."

"We want to find Mei," Ivy said eagerly. "Wouldn't it be fun to see her again?"

"It would be wonderful," her grandmother agreed. "You girls might want to check up in the storage room. I already cleared out most of the old things when I gave those bags of clothes to Gladrags, but there's a trunk in the corner. I've saved old letters and cards over the years, and the one I received from Mei might be in there, too. Maybe it will have her address on it."

Up in the top-floor storage room, Ivy opened the battered wooden trunk. Inside were a few photo albums, some folded curtains, and two shoe boxes full of cards and letters.

The girls went through the photo albums first. "Look," said Ivy, pointing, "there's my mom when she was a little girl. And look at Gung Gung with black hair!" As they turned the pages, Ivy translated the handwritten characters labeling the photos, but none of the captions mentioned anyone named Mei Meng.

The first shoe box held business receipts from the early days of the restaurant. There were clippings from both Chinese- and English-language newspapers, with reviews of the

Happy Panda. The second box held Christmas cards, birthday cards, and letters to Po Po and Gung Gung dating back many years. The girls laughed at the sentimental birthday greetings, and looked at photos of unfamiliar people enclosed in some of the cards. Some of the messages were in English, but most were in Chinese. There was, however, no mention of anyone named Mei Meng. Ivy did find a birthday card to Gung Gung from someone named Wura Meng and a few letters from people named Meng Wah and Mei Chong Wu. And Julie found a Christmas card with a fat snowman riding a cable car, signed simply "Mei and Robert, Christmas 1932." That card had a faded snapshot of a fat baby tucked into it. Julie laughed and showed the photo to Ivy.

"This little guy looks as roly-poly as the snowman!"

Ivy turned the photo over and translated the faded handwritten characters: "Baby Billy growing fast. Has learned to walk already!"

Julie chuckled, but she was disappointed that

the trunk hadn't revealed anything useful in their search for Mei Meng.

"Let's take all the cards and letters with the names Mei and Meng in them, and we'll ask Po Po which one is her old friend," suggested Ivy. "Too bad she didn't keep the envelopes so we'd have the return addresses."

Julie shook out the folded curtains, hoping to find something useful—an old paper with Mei Meng's address and phone number, perhaps—but nothing flew out. Regretfully, she replaced the curtains and closed the trunk. She stood up and brushed the dust off the knees of her jeans.

"Let's get a snack," said Ivy. "Po Po's dumplings are out of this world."

"We'll drown our sorrows in dumplings," Julie agreed. She squared her shoulders. "But even if none of those cards came from Mei Meng, we aren't done trying. Somehow we need to get ourselves over to Angel Island."

9
PIECES OF THE PUZZLE

The cook gave them each a bowl of fragrant dumplings, and the girls took their snack into the restaurant's dining room. They found Ivy's grandfather seated at a booth, enjoying a pot of tea while going over the account ledgers. Gung Gung peered at them over his reading glasses. "I hear you've got your doll back," he said to Julie. "I am so glad to hear it."

"Yes, I found her in the alley behind the bakery," said Julie, taking Yue Yan out of her jacket to show Gung Gung. "And it looks as if someone took off her head, too, but then popped it back on. And she's all dirty—but I think my mom can help me fix her up again."

Gung Gung examined the doll carefully. "I think she will be fine," he said gravely. Then he looked at Ivy. "So you've been up in the storage room? What have you discovered?"

"Just these old cards," Ivy said, laying them on the table in front of him. "Do you know if one of these is from Mei Meng?"

Gung Gung glanced at the cards. "Well, Meng Wah and Mei Chong Wu used to be our neighbors before they moved to Seattle. I don't know Wura Meng or Mei and Robert. You will have to ask Po Po about those two. But she is resting now. She needs her nap in the afternoon in order to be fresh for the evening customers." He stretched his arms over his head. "I could use a little shut-eye myself for an hour."

"We're going to head home now," Ivy said. "But, Gung Gung, do you think you could take us to Angel Island sometime soon? Like maybe after school tomorrow?"

Gung Gung set down his pen and closed his ledger. "Not a good place, that island. Lots of bad memories. And you will not find Mei there, I assure you."

Julie was startled by his sharp tone. "Oh, we

know that!" she said. "But there could be information on Angel Island about people who were detained there. We might learn something to lead us to Mei."

"Maybe Po Po will take us," suggested Ivy.

Gung Gung shook his head. "No sense bringing up the past. Water under the bridge. That island is the last place Po Po should visit. But I'll ask her about the people who sent these cards. Be careful riding home, girls."

It was clear they'd been dismissed. Ivy kissed her grandfather on his weathered cheek, and both girls said good-bye. They took their bikes and set off.

But Julie wasn't done trying to get to the island. "I'll ask my parents," she murmured to Ivy as the girls rode home.

"And I'll phone Po Po later," said Ivy, "and let her decide for herself if she wants to go back to Angel Island!"

❀

Julie broached the subject with her dad as he drove her and Tracy back to their apartment that Sunday evening.

"Sorry, Jules," he said. "Tomorrow I'll be on a plane to England." His broad smile didn't look sorry at all. "Granted, England's on an island, too, so maybe we'll both be island-hopping this week."

Julie sighed. Her dad was always cheerful before a big trip. She leaned her head against the car window in the backseat and stared out at the darkening streets, hugging Yue Yan. A light drizzle of rain misted the glass.

"It's supposed to rain all week," Tracy commented from the front seat.

"We need it," said Mr. Albright. Then he started talking about how in England it rained every week, sometimes for days on end, and the whole country as a result was lush and green, unlike California, where rain was precious and rare except in winter. The hills turned green in winter but were dusty brown and dry the rest of the year.

Julie fretted, listening. Would the ferry to Angel Island be running if it rained all week? Would her mom take her? Probably not, with the shop so busy and Olivia Kaminsky arriving soon. "What about you, Trace? Please?" begged Julie.

"Sorry, Julie," Tracy replied. "The Valentine Disco committee meets after school every day this week. The dance is Saturday, and we don't have a lot of time to get ready. I'll drop you off at Fisherman's Wharf, though, if you arrange to meet Ivy and her parents there."

But Julie knew it was no use asking Ivy's parents, either. Ivy's dad worked two jobs, and Ivy's mom was in law school. Their weekdays were always packed.

Julie stroked Yue Yan's black hair. She felt too curious now about what had happened to Mei Meng to give up the search for her. She hoped Po Po felt the same way. Po Po was their only chance to get to Angel Island anytime soon, but what if she felt as Gung Gung did—that Angel Island was the last place she'd want to visit?

❖

Just before bedtime that night, Ivy phoned Julie with good news. "Po Po will take us!"

"Oh, that's great!" Julie said. She felt a surge of excitement.

"She said something interesting," Ivy added. "When I told her that Gung Gung was worried the island would upset her, she sort of laughed and said that sometimes it's good to see where we came from in order to appreciate how lucky we are to be where we are now. And she said the past can be like a chain, holding us in place."

Julie thought about that. Did Po Po feel held in place by a chain no one could see? Would a visit to Angel Island release that chain?

"Po Po also told me that the Christmas card signed 'Mei and Robert' is the one from her friend Mei!" Ivy announced. "Po Po said that card was the last she ever heard from her. She doesn't remember their last name, so it won't help us find her after all."

"But now at least we know Mei got married and had a baby by 1932." Julie felt glad the young, frightened girl detained on Angel Island had been able to build a new life in America.

That night, lying in bed with Yue Yan tucked in snugly next to her, Julie listened to raindrops pattering against her window. She thought about Po Po and Mei Meng when they were just girls Tracy's age, lying sleepless in a dormitory on Angel Island, far from home, without their families. She looked around her small, cozy bedroom, and she thought about Olivia Kaminsky, how Olivia would soon have this familiar view while Julie lay on the sleepover mattress on the floor of Tracy's room.

By the light filtering into the room from the streetlamp outside, Julie could see her other dolls sitting in a row on top of the bookcase by the window. Their shiny glass eyes seemed to wink back at her.

10
ANGEL ISLAND

At school on Monday, Julie's friends Joy and Carla made plans to get ice cream after school. They wanted Julie to join them, but she shook her head. "I'm meeting Ivy."

"Bring Ivy along," Carla suggested.

"Thanks, but we're going to Angel Island with Ivy's grandmother," Julie told them. She started to tell her friends all the events of the past weekend. But so much had happened, she'd only just described first finding the coaching note when Mrs. Duncan, their fifth-grade teacher, clapped her hands for silence.

Julie took out her math book, but her thoughts were not on fractions and decimals. She was wondering whether their trip to Angel Island would help them finally figure out what had become of Po Po's dear friend, Mei Meng.

As soon as the final bell rang for the day, Julie waved good-bye to her friends and hurried to the corner where Tracy planned to pick her up. She hoped Tracy would not waste time gabbing with boys after school.

She was on time! Julie jumped into the car with a grin. "Full steam ahead!"

Tracy turned the radio up loud, and both girls sang along with the Bee Gees.

"I can't wait for the Valentine Disco," Tracy said over the blaring music as they neared Fisherman's Wharf. She pulled neatly up to the curb and turned down the music. "Okay, here you are. Look—Ivy and her grandmother are already here." She pointed at the ticket booth.

Julie saw Po Po, looking small in her heavy winter coat and bright red scarf, sitting on a bench. Ivy stood in line for tickets.

Julie left her school book bag with Tracy but took out the wallet containing money her mom had given her for the fare. She zipped it into her jacket pocket. "Thanks for driving me, Tracy. See you later!"

"Bon voyage!" Tracy drove away with a little toot of the horn.

Julie hurried over to Ivy and Po Po, excitement mounting as they waited in line to board the passenger ferry to Angel Island. On board, Ivy and Julie settled Po Po in an indoor seat, and then they climbed the steep stairs and pushed through the narrow door to the upper deck. A cold, salty wind whipped their hair into tangles. They pressed against the railing and watched the roiling sea below them as the ferry pulled out of the dock.

"Think of Po Po and Mei Meng standing on the deck like this, coming to Angel Island all those years ago," said Ivy dreamily.

Julie could imagine how it might have felt, sailing through the opening called the "golden gate" into San Francisco Bay. She watched as they approached the dark shape of Angel Island. It was a large hill covered with trees.

Clustered near the water were the buildings of the Immigration Station.

As they disembarked at the visitors' center and began the long walk to the buildings, Julie glanced at Ivy's grandmother. How strange it must feel for Po Po to return to the place she had once stayed as a girl, Julie reflected as they approached the Immigration Station. She shivered and looked around at the abandoned structures. It was all too easy to imagine young Jiao Jie and Mei sitting inside, staring out the windows—waiting, waiting, waiting—unsure whether they would be admitted to this strange new country.

A tour guide wearing the uniform of a state park ranger gathered a group outside a large, dilapidated building. "This was the detention barracks," she informed them. "After World War Two, it was abandoned and fell into disrepair. It was scheduled for destruction in 1970." She pointed at the hulking building, and her voice rose dramatically. "But just before it was to be demolished, a park ranger discovered calligraphy carved into the walls—poems written in Chinese!"

"Yes," whispered Po Po. "I remember..."

"Mr. Long mentioned those," Julie murmured.

"The poems were sad ones, full of loss and longing and frustration," the ranger continued. "'How was anyone to know that my dwelling place would be a prison?'" She quoted the lines of poetry softly. "Today the poems remind us that this place was an important part of Chinese American history. After the poems were discovered, people formed a committee to save the immigration buildings. One day we hope to turn them into a museum."

Julie wanted to ask the ranger if there were records of the detainees kept here on the island. But Ivy and her grandmother moved away from the group, so Julie followed. She walked just behind them as they wandered among the empty shells of buildings. Around the side of the barracks, Po Po paused. "This is where we played," she told the girls in a tremulous voice. "Mei and I. The women and children were allowed to walk outdoors once a week, and the men had to stay in an enclosure. Mei and I played tag. It felt so good to run after being cooped up indoors!"

"Over there," Po Po said, pointing, "was where we ate. Such bad food it was! Just thin soup and rice, dry bread and tea. Sometimes a slice of beef or fish. How I longed for fresh vegetables or a nice piece of fruit!"

After the tour, Po Po seemed tired. "I'll sit here and wait for the ferry," she told the girls when they'd returned to the dock. Seating herself on a bench, she gave permission for Julie and Ivy to walk down to the beach. In the distance, the girls could see buildings and towns on the shoreline across the bay. *How frustrating it must have been for Po Po and Mei, stuck here on this island, looking out at this view,* thought Julie— *freedom so close and yet so far away.*

"Here comes the ferry," Ivy said, pointing. "We'd better go back up to the dock."

The ranger walked over to say good-bye as they waited to board. "Thanks for the tour," Ivy said with a shy smile. "It was really fascinating."

"Yes, thanks a lot," Julie chimed in.

"You're welcome," the young ranger said, looking pleased. Then she glanced over her shoulder at Ivy's grandmother. "I'm not so sure everyone in this group enjoyed the visit. For some, memories can be painful."

"I recently learned that my grandmother was detained here," said Ivy softly. "I can't believe she'd never mentioned it before."

"Oh, I can understand that," said the park ranger. "Detainees here felt the injustice of their situation keenly. All other immigrants were allowed to enter America freely. Only the Chinese were excluded. There was even an act of Congress to keep them out called the Chinese Exclusion Act!"

That's what Lonny Wu was talking about, Julie thought, glancing at Ivy. Her friend's face was flushed.

"It must have been so scary for the children who were traveling alone," said Julie.

"Like my grandmother and the friend she

met on the ship," murmured Ivy. "In fact, we're trying to reunite them."

"But we don't know how to find the friend," explained Julie. "Her name was Mei Meng. We know she married somebody called Robert and had a baby named Billy. Are there any records here on the island that would give us an address of where she went to live?"

"There are no records like that available to the public," said the young woman regretfully. "But you might try checking old newspaper archives at the public library. See if there's some mention of her in any announcements of births, marriages, or deaths."

"Oh, I hope she's not dead," Ivy murmured.

The girls said good-bye to the ranger and went to sit with Po Po. Gulls flapped overhead, screaming to each other. Julie could see the ferry's foaming wake rocking smaller boats on the bay. How would it feel to be on a big boat for weeks, as Jiao Jie and Mei had been?

"Were you seasick on the ship from China?" Julie asked Po Po.

Po Po turned her gaze from the choppy water of the bay to look up the rise behind them—at the barracks. "No, dear. Only homesick. And … heartsick." Ivy squeezed her grandmother's arm sympathetically.

Julie watched as the passenger ferry docked and a sailor moored it with ropes. Passengers lined up to disembark. The people who had already toured the island waited to board for the short ride back to San Francisco.

Julie watched several dozen people stream down the gangplank. Suddenly she gasped and grabbed Ivy's arm. "Look!" she cried, pointing. A woman with her dark hair wrapped in a jade green scarf was walking across the dock.

"Oh—it's Mrs. Chan! With Paul. What a coincidence!" Ivy lifted her arm to wave.

Julie pulled her arm down. "It's not a coincidence," she hissed. "Don't let them see us." She pulled Ivy away from the bench.

"Why not?" demanded Ivy.

"Don't you think it's really strange that Mrs. Chan is here?" Julie asked in a low voice. "She doesn't want us asking questions—'pestering people,' she called it, and 'playing detective'— but here she is on Angel Island!"

"You mean you think she's playing detective herself?" asked Ivy.

Julie narrowed her eyes in thought. "Well, she does collect dolls. And she teaches Chinese school in the building near where we found Yue Yan!"

Ivy looked dubious. "And now she's following us to Angel Island? But why?"

"I'm not quite sure," Julie said slowly. "I'm just noticing things."

Ivy tilted her head, considering. "It's hard to picture Mrs. Chan sneaking upstairs while the rest of us were eating dinner. Besides, wasn't she sitting with us the whole time? And even if she *did* go into the apartment, the minute she saw our dolls, she'd have known they weren't old or valuable—because she's a doll collector! There'd be no reason for her to steal them."

Julie knew that Ivy was right, yet she couldn't shake the image of Mrs. Chan carefully studying the old coaching note that told of a doll bringing riches...

Ivy stepped away from Julie and greeted Mrs. Chan in Chinese as the woman approached.

Mrs. Chan nodded to them and replied in Chinese to Ivy. Then she switched to English. "I guess I shouldn't be surprised to see you here!" she said cordially. "After hearing your grandmother's story, I think everyone will be interested in seeing Angel Island. I've never been over here. But ever since you found that coaching note, Julie, I can't get the place out of my head. It must be absolutely full of fascinating history."

Julie listened suspiciously to Mrs. Chan. She tried to imagine the teacher sneaking upstairs... stealing the dolls. She had to admit it was an improbable scenario. And yet *someone* had stolen the dolls. Someone had tossed Yue Yan away—right behind the Chinese school. Someone had pulled the dolls' heads off, popping Yue Yan's head on backward and leaving Li Ming's plastic head in the trash.

*Wait a minute. The thief pulled **both** the dolls' heads off,* Julie thought. *Why?*

The words of the coaching note came back to her: *She will bless you with riches.*

Julie's own scalp prickled. Something was starting to make sense. If the thief had meant to steal *Kai*—had meant to pull off *Kai's* head... was it to see if something was *inside* Kai? Something *valuable*?

As Mrs. Chan moved on to speak to Po Po, Julie clutched Ivy's arm. "The jade necklace!" she whispered.

"What do you mean?" asked Ivy.

Julie pulled her friend aside. "It makes sense to me now! The person who stole Li Ming thought the jade necklace was hidden inside her. You know, the jade necklace your grandmother was supposed to give to her father."

"The one she didn't give him..." Ivy's voice trailed off. "Because she didn't have it."

"Right." Julie nodded. Excitement mounted inside her. She just knew she was on the right track; suddenly the theft and the pulled-off heads were all making sense. "Whoever took our dolls hoped one of them had something hidden inside."

"I see what you mean," Ivy said excitedly. "Po Po's mother wouldn't have wanted to entrust such a valuable thing to a girl traveling alone. She wrote in the note that Jiao Jie should give the doll to her father—which is a strange thing to say, really, unless the doll had something in it that the father would want."

"Exactly!" Julie strode forward to be first in line for the ferry. "I want to get to those newspaper archives. I think we're not the only ones looking for Mei. We've got to find her before anyone else does. We need to see if she still has that old doll."

"And if she does?" asked Ivy.

Julie looked around to be sure that she could not be overheard. She lowered her voice to a whisper. "We open it up, of course. And see what's inside."

11
ALIVE AND KICKING

The girls resolved not to mention their theory to Po Po unless they found Mei—and Kai, the rag doll. Julie was itching to go to the public library and start checking the newspaper archives, but her mom kept her busy at home that evening cleaning out her closet, her desk, and her bedside table so that Olivia Kaminsky would have space for her own things.

Tuesday morning the phone rang. "Can you get that, Julie?" Mrs. Albright called.

Julie drained the last of her orange juice and reached for the phone on the wall. "Hello?"

"Good mornin', Joyce darlin'!" a raspy voice caroled exuberantly.

Julie held the receiver away from her ear. "Just a minute. I'll get her."

"Now hold on just a sec, babydoll! Can this be Miss Tracy? Or—what's the little one's name? Little Miss Julie?"

Julie sighed. "Yes, this is Julie." She felt a sinking sensation in her belly, as if the cereal she'd just eaten had turned to stone.

"Hello there, sweet treasure! Can you guess who this is?"

"No," Julie said curtly. "Hold on, please. I'll get my mom." Hastily she put the phone on the table and went to the bathroom, where her mom stood before the mirror, helping Tracy fix her hair. "Phone for you."

Julie went back to her room to get her book bag. She glanced around at the unmade bed, pajamas lying in a heap on the floor, scattered papers from her attempts at writing a book report. From the kitchen she could hear her mom's laughter.

"I can't wait, Olivia! We'll see you on Saturday."

Julie knew she should clean up her room, but why bother? It wasn't her room anymore, not really. Only till Saturday. She was glad she didn't have to come straight home today after school for more cleaning. Last night her mom and Ivy's mom had talked by phone and agreed that the girls could meet at the public library after school. At last, she and Ivy could search the archives.

At school, during lunch in the cafeteria, Julie told Joy and Carla all about the invasion of Olivia Kaminsky. She imitated Olivia's loud, raspy voice. "Please pass me a napkin, babydoll," she trilled to Joy. "Would you like this extra cookie, sweet treasure?" she brayed to Carla.

Her friends laughed, and Julie laughed with them, but inside her stomach the stone sat hard and heavy.

After school, in a light drizzle, she rode the bus to the library. Ivy was waiting just inside the door. They stopped at the information desk to ask for directions to the newspaper archives and then climbed the stairs to the third floor. There, a helpful young librarian, his hair worn in an exuberant Afro, showed them how to use the microfilm machines. "Old newspapers preserved on film can last for five hundred years if properly stored," he told them. "It's a great way of saving history."

"We're trying to track down an old friend of my grandmother's," Ivy explained. "So we thought we'd look at old newspapers to see if her name is mentioned anywhere."

"Good plan," the man said, nodding. "What time span are we talking about?"

"Well, 1919 would be the earliest, because that's when she first came here from China."

The librarian gave a low whistle. "That's over fifty years of film. It'll take forever. Is there a way of narrowing your search?"

Julie thought a moment. "We know she got married to a man named Robert sometime before 1932. She sent a Christmas card that year with a note about her husband and baby."

"And we know she was about fourteen or fifteen in 1919," said Ivy.

"Good," said the librarian. "Then look at the wedding announcements starting in 1924 or

1925, which is when she'd have been about twenty years old."

Opening a box containing microfilm of the *San Francisco Chronicle*, he showed them how to load the microfilm reels onto the spindles, close the glass plate, and turn the crank to advance or rewind. Once the girls had the knack of it, he left them alone in the quiet room.

Silence stretched out as the girls read the old print. They wrote down all the people named Mei or Meng in a notebook, and at the end of an hour they had a small list. There was a Mei-Mei Chung marrying Waldo Li in 1924. There was a Marion Meng marrying Ling Chen in 1926. There was a listing for a Mei Xan marrying Robert Liu in 1927. They also found Jane Meng marrying Richard Compton Jones in 1927, and Bessie-Beulah Meng marrying James Chang in 1928.

"Whoa," said Julie, grinning. "How would you like to be named Bessie-Beulah?"

"No thanks," Ivy said. "But look—there's just one Robert. Robert Liu!"

"Yes, but he married someone called Mei Ex-an," Julie faltered.

"It's pronounced *Zan*," Ivy told her.

Julie read the entire notice aloud: "The wedding of Miss Mei Xan of Oakland and Mr. Robert Liu of this city was solemnized in San Francisco on Saturday, May 7th, 1927, at the home of the groom's parents, Mr. and Mrs. Ching Lei Liu. The couple will reside in Oakland."

"Mei came to America as a paper daughter," Ivy pointed out. "I wonder if she took her new family's last name?"

"Of course! That makes sense. Ivy, you're a genius!" Julie paused. "Hey—remember the Christmas card photo? Baby Billy learning to walk?"

"What about it?"

"If we check the birth announcements and find an announcement that Mei and Robert Liu had a baby named Billy, then we'll know for sure it's her!"

They returned to the microfilm files, reading

through all the birth announcements between 1927, when the Lius had married, and 1932.

"Listen to this: 'Robert and Mei Liu joyously announce the birth of their son, William Stuart, January 10, 1932. Six pounds, six ounces,'" Julie read aloud.

"And Billy is a nickname for William," Ivy said excitedly.

Julie copied the information into her notebook. She felt sure they were on the right track for finding Po Po's old friend. As long as Mei Meng was Mei Xan...

"So now what?" asked Ivy.

"The phone book, I think," said Julie. "To look up Mei Liu."

"Oh, Julie, what if they moved to New York or somewhere?"

They found the librarian and told him what they had discovered. "I'm impressed," he said, directing them to the telephone books. "You'll find listings for all of California here."

Julie opened the thick Oakland telephone directory and thumbed through it eagerly.

"We just need to find the name Mei, Robert, or William," she said. "Or any of those initials."

"Or nicknames," Ivy reminded her.

There was a whole column of Lius but none named Mei. There were no Roberts, either, but there were two listings with the initial R, three Williams, one Billy, and an initial B. Julie wrote down all the phone numbers in her notebook. Then they looked in the San Francisco phone book as well and found another column of Lius, among them three listed as Rob, one Bill, one Willy, and one just plain M.

Julie wrote down all the names and numbers. Then she and Ivy thanked the librarian and left. "The Happy Panda isn't too far from here," Ivy pointed out. "My mom can pick us up there."

The two girls hurried toward Chinatown, up one hilly street and down another. It was raining now, and Julie wished she had an umbrella. Panting slightly, they soon stepped, dripping, into the restaurant through the back door. The cook greeted them with towels to dry their wet hair and said that Gung Gung and Po Po were around the corner having a cup of tea with Mr. Long, but they should be back soon.

Ivy led the way upstairs to her grandparents' apartment, to the phone on the living room table. "Okay," she said. "I'll start." She dialed the first number.

Julie held her breath.

The first R. Liu they reached sounded like an old man. But his name was Reginald, he said, and he had never been married and didn't want to be married. The second R. Liu was named Richard, and he didn't want to buy whatever they were selling. The next person they phoned was a third-grader in Oakland named Billy Liu, and his father was named Billy Liu, too, and they had just moved to California from Nebraska, and since his dad wasn't home from work yet and his mom was busy with the baby, would they help with his math homework?

"Is your mom—um, no, wait; is your grand-mother named Mei?" asked Ivy. "Is anybody in your family named Mei?"

"Nope. My grandma is named Edna."

Several W. Lius did not answer their phones, and one number had been disconnected. With a sigh, Ivy handed the receiver to Julie. "You try," she said. "This is depressing. What if Mei got divorced and remarried and is living right nearby, but with a different last name? Or . . . what if she's dead?"

"Don't give up yet." Julie took the receiver. "There are still two to call in Oakland and a bunch more here in San Francisco. Just think how happy Po Po will be if we can find her old friend. And maybe Mei still has Kai!" She curled the phone cord around her hand and dialed the next number.

"Hello?" The deep voice sounded distracted. "Liu residence."

"Is this Mr. Liu?" Julie asked, as she'd asked each time. "Mr. Robert Liu? Or Mr. William Liu?"

"Who is this?"

Julie took a deep breath. "I'd like to speak with Mei," she said. "Mei Liu, I mean. If her name used to be Mei Meng, or maybe Mei Xan."

There was a silence and then an impatient laugh. "What's this all about? Are you calling for Deanna?"

"Uh, no. I'm trying to find an old friend of my friend's grandmother." Julie winced. That sounded so complicated.

"A friend of your friend's grandmother?" repeated the man doubtfully. "Look, I don't have time for prank calls."

"I'm sorry—really, this isn't a prank! There was a girl named Jiao Jie, who was friends with a girl named Mei Meng back in 1919. That was the year they both came on a ship from China—"

"Okay, hold on, hold on," the man said, and now his voice was no longer skeptical. "My mother's original name was Mei Meng, and she did come from China—in 1919, in fact. So tell me again who you are?"

But Julie countered with another question. "Is your father's name Robert?"

"It was Robert, yes," the man said cautiously.

"And were you born in 1932?"

"I was," replied the man. "But who wants to know—and why?"

"It's him!" Julie hissed to Ivy, turning away from the receiver. "It's the baby!"

"What baby?" asked the man on the other end of the line. He sounded exasperated.

"Sorry," apologized Julie, removing her hand and speaking into the phone again. "But is...is your mother still alive?" She crossed her fingers, hoping.

"Alive and kicking," the man said with a sudden chuckle.

Julie smiled so hard, she felt sure he could feel it through the phone. "In that case," she said, "we'd like to reunite your mother with an old friend!"

12
TEA CAKES AND CONVERSATION

Julie held the phone so that Ivy could hear, too, as the man told the girls that his mother, Mei, had arrived on Angel Island as a paper daughter and had gone to live with her new parents, the Xans. She grew up in Oakland with the family who claimed her as their own, changing her last name to theirs. Then later, Mei married Robert Liu and had a son—Bill himself, the man who was talking to them. Robert had died five years ago, so Mei was now a widow.

"Mom and Dad lived in Chinatown for many years," Mr. Liu said, "but we moved to the Oakland hills when I was in high school. Mom was still living there, alone, until she fell a few weeks ago and broke her hip. She's in a convalescent hospital just now and is very weak, I'm afraid. But meeting your friend's grandmother might perk her up. How enterprising of you to track her down." He asked for Po Po's phone number and said he would get in touch with her himself to arrange a reunion.

Julie thanked him and said good-bye. Then she hung up and flopped onto the couch. "We did it!" she cheered.

"Let's go tell Po Po!" Ivy said. "Before Mr. Liu phones."

The girls grabbed an umbrella from the stand near the door and made their way out of the restaurant and around the corner to Mr. Long's teahouse. Po Po and Gung Gung were seated at a corner table, chatting and sharing a plate of tea cakes. "It is nice to eat in somebody else's restaurant," Gung Gung said when he saw the girls. "Let someone else do the cooking!"

Mrs. Wu set a fresh pot of aromatic tea in front of Po Po, whisking the empty pot away.

"Please join us, girls," said Po Po. "Two more cups, please, Mrs. Wu."

Her dark eyes flashing with excitement, Ivy

began telling her grandparents about their search for Mei Meng and how they had located her son, Bill Liu. Mrs. Wu served the girls their tea, smiling as she heard the story of their successful search.

Po Po listened intently. "I am very touched," she told them, placing her hand on her heart. "Right here. You are very kind girls to look so hard for my old friend."

"We will look forward to meeting her," said Gung Gung. "And to hearing what she has made of herself in the Gold Mountain!" He smiled at the girls, but his eyes were distant, as if seeing back over many years. "It was not easy to be a newcomer here. Many people saw the immigrants from Angel Island as unwelcome intruders. Let us hope that Mei has a happy tale to tell us about her life in California."

At his mention of unwelcome intruders, Julie felt a stab of dismay. A quick glance at her watch confirmed that she was supposed to be home by now, cleaning her room for Olivia Kaminsky's invasion. But before she could ask

to use the phone to call Tracy for a ride, Mr.
Long swept over to their table with another
plate of tea cakes.

"On the house!" he announced. "To celebrate
the reunion of old friends from the ship!"

Julie and Ivy exchanged a wry glance. How
had he heard their news so fast? Julie glanced
over at Mrs. Wu, who was wiping clean a table
on the other side of the room. Clearly, the waitress was as good as a loudspeaker for passing
on the latest news updates.

The bell over the door rang as a new customer entered, and Mr. Long hurried over to
greet him. As he showed the newcomer to a seat
by the window, Julie kicked Ivy's ankle under
the table. "Motorbike man," she hissed.

He unbuckled his helmet and pulled it off to
reveal long black hair tied back in a windblown
ponytail.

"I think you must never work, boy," joked
Mr. Long. "Here in the morning and again in
the afternoon—always buzzing about on that
scooter, or in here wanting my tea cakes!"

"Can I help it if you make the best tea cakes in San Francisco?" The tall young man laughed. He nodded to the girls and Ivy's grandparents at the next table. "I come in here on study breaks," he told them. He stretched out his long legs and accepted the cup of tea Mrs. Wu brought him. "Ahh, there's nothing better."

Julie watched him, surprised that the others seemed so at ease with this stranger.

Carefully stepping over his feet in their big black leather boots, Mrs. Wu smiled at him. "You're a hardworking fellow, Jimmy. I hope my Lonny will think about going on to college like you someday. Will you talk to him about it?"

"Sure," the young man with the ponytail— Jimmy—said easily.

"What are you studying?" Julie asked, her voice suspicious. Ivy elbowed her, but the young man just smiled.

"I'm getting a degree in history."

"Jimmy Yep is one smart boy," Mr. Long told them, clapping the young man on the back. "He moved here all the way across the country from New York to go to school. He's writing a master's thesis about Chinese immigration to America. Isn't that right, Jimmy?"

"Sure is. And maybe I'll even turn it into a book someday. I've been living with my aunt and uncle above their car repair shop—you know Yep's Garage? Being right here in Chinatown is a huge help for my research. I'm getting firsthand accounts from people who immigrated." He turned to Po Po. "Your story about Angel Island was fascinating, Mrs. Sun."

"I noticed you were listening that day at the restaurant," Julie said. "And then you started following us around—"

He gave her a quizzical look. "Following you? I've seen you girls around while I've been interviewing some of the old-timers, but *following you?* Why would I do that?"

Ivy nudged Julie again, and this time she kept silent. If he had been hoping they'd lead him to Mei Meng and her rag doll, then he was doing a good job of bluffing. If he had nothing to do with the stolen dolls, then it was only coincidence they'd seen him so many times. How could she tell which was true? Certainly Po Po and Gung Gung did not seem suspicious of the young man. Gung Gung was asking Jimmy about the classes he was taking, and Po Po was telling him to stop by at the restaurant again. "Come before we get busy with the lunch crowd," she said. "That's the best time to talk. I'm very happy to give you an interview for your book."

Julie felt something shift inside her. Was nothing as it seemed? She stood up abruptly, feeling slightly off balance. "May I use your phone?" she asked Mr. Long. "I need to call my sister and see if she can pick me up. It's late—"

"I can take you home," said Gung Gung. "Both you girls. Save your mothers a drive."

After saying good-bye to everyone, Julie and Ivy followed Gung Gung out of the teahouse and around the corner to his car, parked in the darkening alley behind the Happy Panda. As Gung Gung drove down the steep street, Julie saw Mrs. Chan walking along, her trademark green scarf wrapped around her head against the drizzle. The teacher's head was down, as if she was deep in thought. But she looked up sharply as they passed.

❀

When they pulled up in front of Gladrags, Julie thanked Gung Gung for the ride and then darted inside. She could hear the roar of the vacuum cleaner even before she opened the apartment door.

"I'm home!" she yelled in the doorway.

Mrs. Albright flipped the switch on the vacuum cleaner. "About time," she said wearily. "There's still a lot to do before our guest arrives."

"Sorry, Mom. I went to the library with Ivy, remember? It—our research took a little longer than we expected."

"Please wipe your feet." Mom sighed. "Look, honey, I understand that reuniting Ivy's grandmother with her old friend is important to you right now, but *my* old friend is arriving on

Saturday night, and your room is not ready for her. As soon as you've had some dinner, please finish cleaning out your dresser."

Julie nodded, but she couldn't help thinking that her mother just didn't understand. It was important to find Mei—and to find Po Po's old doll. Someone else was after Kai, and the thief wasn't going to wait around for Julie to finish cleaning out her dresser for Olivia Kaminsky.

13
INTRUDER!

The very next day, Ivy called to say that Po Po had reached Mei by phone at the convalescent hospital and was thrilled that she recognized her old friend's voice. "It's so exciting!" Ivy said. "Mei and her son Bill have invited Po Po and Gung Gung to visit on Friday afternoon. And they've invited both of us to come, too!"

❀

Finally Friday arrived. Julie couldn't stop checking the classroom clock. She groaned when Mrs. Duncan reminded her that there was a student council meeting after school. Julie, as president, couldn't miss the meeting. But she did have the power to make it a short meeting, and at last it was time to meet Ivy and her grandparents for the journey to Oakland. After the BART commuter train crossed the city, it descended into the tunnel beneath the bay. Julie stared out the window at the blackness and shivered a little to think of all that water on top of them.

The train finally emerged into daylight and, after a couple of stops, pulled into the Rockridge station. As they stepped out onto the platform, a lanky Asian man raised his hand in a wave. "Hello!" he called in a friendly voice. "I'm Bill Liu!" He shook hands all around and then motioned for a tall, slender girl to join them.

She was about Julie's and Ivy's age, with long black hair tied into two ponytails. "This is my daughter, Deanna," Mr. Liu said.

Gung Gung bowed and introduced himself and Po Po and the girls. "Thank you for meeting us," he said.

"Thank you for coming! This is very exciting." Mr. Liu led the way out to the street. "I think we'll all fit in our station wagon. It's not far to the convalescent hospital."

"We're hoping to convince Gran to come live with us when she's out of the hospital," Deanna volunteered shyly. "But she loves her own place." Then she put her hand on her dad's arm. "We need to stop by Gran's house, Dad. Remember?" Then to the others she explained, "Gran asked me to return a pile of her library books before the fines get any higher."

"We'll stop on the way," her dad said. "All right, everyone—pile in!"

Julie and Ivy climbed into the farthest rear seat and sat facing backward as Mr. Liu drove through the busy city streets and then up a narrow road into the Oakland hills. Deanna Liu pointed out the window as Mr. Liu pulled into the driveway of a small house built into a hillside shaded by redwood trees. "This is my grandmother's house. But it's going to be hard for Gran to stay here now. Too many stairs!"

Julie thought the house, built of redwood, seemed almost like a tree house camouflaged in the woods. Steep steps led from the driveway up to a deck that ran around the front and side of the house. The deck was full of flowers in pots and baskets and boxes attached to the railings.

Mr. Liu parked and turned around in his seat. "I didn't bring a key, Dee, but you know where Gran leaves the spare key. Just get her library books and we'll be on our way."

Julie and Ivy exchanged a glance. "Are there a lot?" Julie asked. "We can help."

Deanna shrugged. "I don't know how many books there are, but you can come in with me." She jumped out of the car. "Back in a flash, Dad."

Julie, Ivy, and Deanna clattered up the steep flight of wooden steps to the deck. Deanna reached up into the potted fuchsia hanging from a beam and fished out a hidden key.

"You won't need a key, because it looks like your grandmother forgot to lock up," Julie said, pointing to a window that was wide open. "Or is that for her cat to go in and out?"

Deanna frowned. "Gran doesn't have a cat. And that window shouldn't be open."

INTRUDER!

Julie followed Deanna and Ivy into the house. Deanna walked straight into the living room and shut the window. "There. Now, the library books are in Gran's bedroom." She went past the kitchen and down a hallway lined with shelves. The lower shelves were full of books, but the long top shelf held dolls—exquisitely gowned dolls, with elegant porcelain faces and beautifully styled hair.

"Wow, look at these!" Ivy said eagerly. "Your gran's a doll collector?"

"She sure is," said Deanna with a grin. "She has a doll from just about every country in the world, I think—" She broke off, bending to pick up a doll that was lying on the floor. "How did you get knocked over?"

A thud came from the back of the house. The girls froze.

Then came a scraping sound.

Julie's heart beat hard. "Someone's here!" she hissed.

"We need to get out!" Ivy whispered desperately.

"We need to get my dad!" cried Deanna. She tore back to the front door, flung it open, and bolted onto the deck. Ivy followed. But Julie crept farther down the unfamiliar hallway, past the shelves of dolls, past a small bathroom...

"Dad!" Julie could hear Deanna yelling. "Come quick!"

The sound of breaking glass came from the next room, and a muffled exclamation.

Julie stopped outside the open door of the bedroom, her heart hammering in fear. Slowly she peered through the doorway. She saw a neatly made bed, with covers tucked in tightly. She saw a row of dolls lined up on a bookcase—except for one that was knocked over and three that lay on the floor. The room was empty, and the bedroom window, which looked out onto the long deck, was wide open. A colored glass suncatcher lay in pieces on the wood floor.

Julie rushed across the room and looked out the open window. Down below the raised porch, she saw flashes of green as the intruder crashed through the underbrush and darted around the redwood trees, heading toward the road. The intruder was getting away!

Footsteps pounded down the hall, and Mr. Liu appeared in the doorway. He quickly assessed the situation. "How lucky that my mother wasn't here!" he exclaimed. "I'm going to call the police."

Gung Gung was right behind him. "Julie!" he said. "You should not have stayed in the house. You should have come running out to us with Ivy."

"I'm sorry," said Julie. "I wanted to see—"

"What?" pressed Mr. Liu. He looked at her intently. "Did you see who it was?"

"No, but the person was wearing something green." With a stab of memory, Julie pictured Mrs. Chan's green scarf. And Mrs. Chan collected dolls, too!

Mr. Liu went to the phone on the bedside table but then put down the receiver, shaking his head. "I forgot—there's no service. I had it stopped when my mother moved into the convalescent home last month. Well, let's go to her now, and I'll make a police report from there." He looked around the room. "This is very upsetting, but it doesn't actually look as if anything has been taken. Just some dolls knocked off the shelf, but they aren't damaged. And this stained-glass ornament that my mother had hanging in the window was broken." He bent down and started to pick up the dolls, but then he stopped. "I guess we should leave everything for the police to see," he said slowly.

"I think you girls surprised a would-be thief and scared him off," said Gung Gung proudly. Then she told Mr. Liu and Deanna about the break-in in their own apartment, and about the theft of the girls' dolls.

"More dolls?" Mr. Liu frowned. "What would a thief want with dolls?"

"That's what we've all been wondering," said Po Po.

Julie took a deep breath. "Does Mrs. Liu have one special doll? One old doll?"

"My mother thinks her whole collection is

special," he replied. "Some of these dolls are valuable antiques."

"But does she have a rag doll?" asked Julie.

"How funny you should ask," Deanna said. "Because there is one old doll from China..."

"Where?" Julie pressed.

"Well...I don't see it," said Deanna, looking around. "Gran usually keeps it right there—on the bedside table."

Julie wheeled around. The bedside table held only a lamp and the telephone. She groaned in defeat. The thief had found what he—or she—was looking for.

Mr. Liu reminded Deanna to get the library books she'd originally come for, and they all returned to the car. He drove down the hill and through Oakland to Mrs. Liu's convalescent center near Lake Merritt. Everyone was talking about the intruder, about calling the police—everyone but Julie. She sat in the back of the station wagon, staring out at the streets, and didn't say a word. Her heart was heavy.

How the thief must be gloating now, running

through the wooded lots with Kai clutched tight! How agonizing to get so close, only to have Kai snatched away.

✿

Deanna led the way into the Lakeside Convalescent Hospital, a gracious building in the heart of Oakland just a block from Lake Merritt. The receptionist greeted them.

Mr. Liu quietly told her about the break-in and asked to use her phone. While he was filing the police report, Gung Gung, Po Po, Ivy, and Julie followed Deanna down the wide corridor to her grandmother's room.

"Gran?" Deanna called out, knocking lightly.

A voice called out in Chinese, and everyone but Julie laughed. Deanna translated for Julie. "She says to get in there and be quick about it!"

Po Po led the way into the room. A small Chinese lady lay propped high on pillows in a hospital bed. The elderly women clutched each other's hands and spoke rapidly in Chinese.

Po Po had tears in her eyes. She turned to the others and introduced Gung Gung, and then Ivy and Julie.

"So these are the girls," Mrs. Liu said in English. "What clever girls to reunite old friends after so many years! What a wonderful gift for the Chinese New Year! Now you must all sit down and tell me how you managed it." She reached for the buzzer on her bedside table. "More chairs for my honored guests, please," she told the young nurse who popped her head into the room.

Mr. Liu joined them, and then everyone sat down to listen as Julie told how she'd first found the coaching note. Ivy described the break-in at her grandparents' apartment, and how the girls suspected that their dolls had been taken in error. "We think the thief really wanted the rag doll my grandmother gave you."

Po Po looked at Julie in surprise.

"Little Kai?" Mrs. Liu sounded intrigued. "But why would a thief want her?"

"Well, we *think* we know why," said Julie

slowly. "But now we'll never know for sure, because Kai's been stolen." Her shoulders slumped.

Mrs. Liu raised her eyebrows. "Stolen?" She pursed her lips. "Kai has been my good-luck charm ever since Jiao Jie gave her to me on Angel Island." She looked at Po Po, her eyes crinkled in a smile. "I was so frightened then, and so alone. I even held tight to that doll during my interview. And she came along with me when at last I met the family I had to pretend was my own." She reached out and gripped Po Po's hand. "Kai was the best good-luck gift! And she was the first doll I ever owned. Over the years I have collected many fancy dolls, but still and always, Kai is the dearest."

"And now she's gone," Julie said softly. "I'm so sorry, Mrs. Liu. If I had run down the hallway faster, I might have seen who took her. And I might have been able to save the treasure."

14
BURIED TREASURE

"Treasure?" Po Po raised her eyebrows.

Ivy looked at Julie. "You tell her."

Julie took a deep breath. "We think the intruder knew about the coaching note and figured out that there was something precious hidden in your doll. That would explain why our dolls were stolen—the thief thought maybe one of them was the doll you had talked about the night we found the coaching note. They were the only dolls in your apartment, after all. That's why the heads were popped off—so the thief could look inside the dolls!"

"Look inside?" Po Po's voice was puzzled.

But Gung Gung cleared his throat. "I wondered about that," he said in a gravelly voice. "But I thought it best not to say anything.

What's done is done, and what's gone is gone."

"I still don't see—" Po Po's brow furrowed.

"Remember the jade necklace, the one your father had asked your mother to bring from China?" Julie said. "We think your mother hid it inside Kai."

Po Po's mouth opened in surprise. "You mean . . . you think she sent the necklace with me but never told me?"

Julie nodded. "I think she wrote it in the coaching note, in a sort of code for your father. But—"

"But I lost the coaching note, and so he never saw it," Po Po finished breathlessly. "Oh my goodness! And now if Kai has been stolen, we'll never know . . ."

Mrs. Liu was shaking her head. "As I told you, I've always kept Kai with me, for luck. And so of course when I came to the hospital for my hip operation, I wouldn't leave her behind, would I?"

Julie turned to the old woman. "You mean she *wasn't* stolen today? You have her here with you?" Julie felt a quiet thrumming inside, like wings of hope beating softly.

"Deanna," said her grandmother, "please pull my suitcase out of that little closet."

They all held their breath as Mrs. Liu's old hands fumbled with the zipper on the small suitcase. At last she withdrew a limp little rag doll with black yarn hair, wearing a faded red dress.

Then she reached over and pressed the buzzer on her intercom. "Nurse? Please bring us a pair of scissors!" She handed the rag doll to Po Po. "My dear Jiao Jie, she's all yours."

But Po Po handed the doll to Julie. "I think you must do the honors, Julie, since you found the coaching note in the first place!"

After glancing at Mrs. Liu for permission, Julie took the scissors from the young nurse. Holding her breath, she carefully snipped the stitches at the side of the doll's neck.

The old seam separated easily. Julie's fingers probed gently inside the doll, just as they had probed inside the lining of the red quilted jacket only a week before, when she'd found the folded piece of paper covered with tiny Chinese characters. She felt a hard lump among the wads of cloth stuffing, and her fingers closed around it. Carefully she tugged out a tightly wrapped ball of cotton wadding and handed it to Po Po.

Po Po unwrapped it with trembling fingers. "Oh my!" she exclaimed, staring down at the lustrous necklace in her lap.

The green stones gleamed. Everyone crowded close. "It's beautiful!" "Amazing!" "I can't believe it!"

"To think it was in there all the time," said Mrs. Liu.

"This is what my father expected my mother to bring him—his family fortune," whispered Po Po. "And because my mother could not come herself, she sent the jewels with me." She reached out a shaky finger to stroke the necklace. "I wish she had told me!"

"But you were a young girl," Gung Gung reminded her. "Your mother was worried about putting you in charge of such a thing. No doubt she thought that hiding it in the doll was the best way to keep it safe."

"It's been so safe that no one has found it in more than fifty years!" Ivy added.

"Practically a lifetime," murmured Mrs. Liu.

Po Po looked out the window at the darkening sky and shook her head. "How we could have used the money this would have brought." Her eyes had a remembering look in them.

"I'm so sorry I never knew it was there," said Mrs. Liu. "Of course I would have tracked you down and returned such a treasure."

"Of course you would have." Po Po sifted the beads of the gleaming necklace between her fingers, and then smiled at her old friend. "My parents meant for this necklace to be sold, and the money was to help us make a good life in our new country. It was very hard at first, and difficult to feel so unwelcome—as if we were intruding into a place where we weren't wanted. But we came anyway, and we made ourselves at home—and we did that even without this treasure!"

Sweet treasure . . . Julie had a sudden memory of Olivia Kaminsky's loud voice in her ear just as Po Po's voice seemed to echo in the room: *It was hard to feel so unwelcome—as if we were intruding into a place where we weren't wanted . . .* Sudden tears came to Julie's eyes.

"I think I know what my parents would want me to do with this necklace now," Po Po said. "They would want me to sell it, as they intended to do themselves. And use the money. We shall do just that, Mei, and share the money."

"Nonsense!" cried Mrs. Liu. "It's your necklace—it doesn't belong to me."

"Really, there's no need," protested Mr. Liu.

But Po Po smiled. "I won't take no for an answer. Half the money must go to Mei because she has been such a good guardian of the doll all these years." She motioned to her purse, near Ivy's chair. "Find my pen, please, Ivy. And my little notebook. I want Mei's phone number and address to make sure we don't lose touch again. This will truly be a wonderful New Year now that I've found my old friend."

Ivy obligingly rummaged in Po Po's capacious handbag. She found a pen and a notebook and gave them to her grandmother, and then she held up a Green Hornet figurine. "Look, Julie, isn't this the little guy Lonny Wu wanted?"

"Hey! It is." Julie stared at the miniature superhero. She felt a sudden prick of unease.

"I can give it to him at Chinese school tomorrow—or at the Valentine Disco," said Ivy.

"Valentine Disco?" asked Deanna. "That sounds fun."

"Yes, and you should come to it with us," Julie said brightly, pushing away the momentary prickle to smile at Deanna. "My sister is helping to organize it. It's a fund-raiser for homeless teens, and families are invited. The high-school kids are going to teach everyone the latest dances." Her smile included Bill Liu, too. "You should all come. In fact, I know my sister is still looking for a few more chaperones."

Mr. Liu laughed. "What an afternoon this has turned out to be. Vandals, long-lost friends, hidden treasures—and now disco dancers?"

"I think a Valentine Disco in San Francisco would be groovy," said Deanna. "Oh, Dad, please say we can go!"

Julie watched the happy scene in the hospital room and knew she should be happy, too. Jiao Jie and Mei Meng were reunited, all the dolls were safe, and the precious jade necklace had been found. But something still kept her feeling off balance.

She walked over to the window and stared out at the hospital parking lot. It was dusk now, and streetlights were coming on. Fog rolled off the bay and blew like ghosts past the window. Somewhere out there, Julie knew, an intruder still lurked.

15

DANCERS—AND ANSWERS

Saturday morning Julie sat at the kitchen table with her mom, who was leafing through a cookbook, deciding what to prepare as a welcome meal for Olivia Kaminsky. Tracy was standing at the counter, rolling out pie crust for the cherry pie she was baking. Julie ate cereal and described the beautiful jade necklace between bites.

"I can't wait to see the necklace," Mom said. "I'm sure Olivia would love to see it, too. We'll take her to the Happy Panda for a meal next week. I know she'll enjoy meeting Ivy's grand-parents." Mom tapped the pencil on the table. "But first I've got to think of what to feed her tonight." She began writing out a grocery list. "Will you girls please make up the bed for

Olivia? I've got to work in the shop. But as soon as Gladrags closes, I'll drop you and Tracy at the dance on my way to the airport."

"Sounds good," said Tracy. She put her pie in the oven. "There! Olivia's favorite pie."

The girls headed to Julie's bedroom. "We should put a few candles on the dresser," said Tracy. "Scented ones, to welcome her."

"Why are you so into Olivia Kaminsky all of a sudden?" demanded Julie. She and her sister were making up the bed in Julie's room with clean, crisp sheets.

"I just think we should give her a chance," Tracy replied, tucking the sheet neatly under the mattress.

"It's going to be awful." Julie pulled up the quilt, frowning.

"Maybe it won't be," said Tracy. She smoothed out the wrinkles. "Mom was telling me how funny Olivia is, and how much they laughed together when they were girls. She said Olivia is a late bloomer who's spent a lot of her life looking after her father. Mom says

Olivia is ready to rocket out on her own—and our place is her launching pad!" Tracy wiggled the pillow deftly into a fresh pillowcase and set it jauntily at the head of the bed. "There, now. All set!"

Tracy left to check on her pie. Julie flopped onto her bed and stared up at the ceiling, soaking up the feeling of her room for one last time before Olivia Kaminsky invaded. The blue bedspread didn't feel as cozy as Julie's own. *Where was **her** bedspread?* Julie wondered. She got up, crossed the hall, and opened the door of Tracy's bedroom—the bedroom they would now share. She stopped, staring.

Tracy was on the floor, kneeling over a big piece of paper. In her hand was a paintbrush. She was finishing a poster—but not for the Valentine Disco. It was a poster for Julie. Tracy had painted a border of stars and moons around the edge of the poster, framing the words *Welcome, Julie!*

Tracy looked over her shoulder. "Hey! You're not supposed to come in here until tonight. Be careful—don't step on it!"

"Wow!" Julie stared down at the poster. "Thanks, Tracy. I know you don't really want to share your room."

"I've decided it might be fun," Tracy said. "And it's only for a month or two." She pointed toward the door with her paintbrush. "Now— out. Don't come in here until the alien invader arrives!"

But Julie didn't leave right away. She looked around Tracy's bedroom. The sleepover mattress in the corner near Tracy's window was now topped with Julie's own India-print bedspread. Next to the bed, Mom had placed a small pink-beaded lamp from Gladrags. Her new place in Tracy's room looked cozy.

Julie wandered back to her own bedroom and stood looking down at the rumpled blue bedspread. She smoothed it out. Would Olivia Kaminsky feel as welcome in this room as Tracy had made Julie feel in hers?

Julie darted back into the hallway and tapped on Tracy's bedroom door. "Hey, Trace?"

she called. "Do you have any extra poster paper? And some paints I can use?"

❀

Julie pushed through the wide double doors into the high-school gymnasium and was immediately engulfed in flashing lights and pounding music. Streamers flew from the basketball hoops, and a bubble machine sent filmy bubbles soaring like little planets above the heads of the dancers. Julie found Ivy and her family by the snack table with Mr. Liu, Deanna, and Deanna's mother, a fashionable woman with a feathered haircut and a firm handshake. "A nice event," she shouted to Julie over the music. "It's great to see people of all ages dancing!"

"I wish Gran could have come," Deanna said. "And Ivy's grandparents."

"Po Po said if we weren't going to do the waltz, she'd better stay home." Ivy grinned.

"Come on," said Julie. "They're teaching everyone the Hustle!" She linked arms with Ivy and Deanna, and they hurried over to join the crowd.

The room pulsed with music. Strobe lights flashed, and the disco ball spun steadily over-head, sending out a circle of stars. A line of teenagers pumped their arms and spun around, teaching everyone else to do the moves.

Julie felt as if she could dance all night. She was blissfully learning the Electric Slide when Tracy grabbed her hand and pulled her out of the line of dancers.

"Mom's here," she said into Julie's ear, "with Olivia."

Julie followed Tracy back to the food table, where their mom was standing with the woman Julie knew must be Olivia Kaminsky. The loud voice on the phone had made Julie imagine her mom's friend as big and bossy. But Olivia was short and plump. Her eyes were bright and kind and, surprisingly, a little shy. Her raspy voice carried easily over the music. "Are these the li'l darlin's?"

"Nice to meet you," Tracy said politely.

Julie smiled. "Hi, I'm Julie," she said over the music.

"You're both perfect angels to let a stranger move in, but I hope you'll put up with me, and we'll all be the best of friends," said Olivia.

"Ready to learn the Funky Chicken?" asked Tracy as a new song started up.

"Dang!" boomed Olivia. "I can't—I mean, I've never—" She looked anxiously out at the dancers.

"I can help you," Julie offered. She felt glad that when their guest entered her new bedroom that night, she'd see a poster lying atop the blue bedspread proclaiming *Welcome, Olivia!*

They moved to the center of the dance floor, where Tracy and the high-school kids were teaching the steps. Olivia Kaminsky proved to be a fast learner.

A wild group of boys led by Paul Chan spun past. Mike Gee and Andrew ran through the dancers, chased by Lonny Wu. Lonny darted nimbly around the dancers.

Julie felt dizzy. The spinning mirror ball was

making Julie's head ache. Somehow the music seemed too loud now. She looked out at the dancers and saw Olivia Kaminsky boogeying with Tracy and Jimmy Yep. She saw Mrs. Chan clapping to the beat.

"Here's the Robot Crunch!" yelled Paul, jerking his arms.

"Hey—here's the Alien Abduction Twirl!" Mike Gee spun wildly.

Lonny Wu laughed. "Cool, man!" He leaped into the air and then rolled on the floor, his green sweater flashing with stars from the mirrored ball. "My new disco move is called the Green Hornet!"

The Green Hornet? Julie's memory flew back to the flashes of green in the redwood trees by Mrs. Liu's house—the intruder running away. Suddenly Julie was sorry she'd ever suspected Ivy's Chinese teacher of stealing Li Ming and Yue Yan.

She strode right over to where Lonny Wu was spinning like a top and stuck out her foot to stop him.

"Hey!" He glared at her.

She put her hands on her hips. "It was you," she shouted over the music.

Lonny spun to face her. "What was me?"

"You know what I'm talking about—" Julie began, but suddenly Lonny shoved past her, running for the double doors.

"Stop!" Julie cried, but only Ivy heard her over the Bee Gees' music. Both girls pelted after Lonny.

Before Lonny got past the doors of the gymnasium, Mr. Liu reached out and caught him. "What's going on here, young man?"

Mr. Liu escorted Lonny out into the hallway. Julie and Ivy followed. "All right, calm down now," Mr. Liu said. "What's this about, Julie?"

"It was Lonny!" Julie cried. "He broke into your mother's house and into Ivy's grandparents' apartment. He stole our dolls!"

Lonny flushed. "You can't prove it." His voice was belligerent, but his eyes looked worried.

"The Green Hornet's supposed to be a *good* guy," Julie snapped.

"Hold on now," said Mr. Liu calmly. "Green Hornet? What's this all about?" He kept his grip on Lonny but held out one hand to Julie. "Take a deep breath and start from the beginning."

"It was the birthday cake that tipped me off," Julie told him. "That leftover piece—remember, Ivy? One of the guests hadn't eaten his cake—or taken his superhero party favor. It didn't seem to mean anything at the time, but later Lonny asked about the figurine, and I realized the uneaten cake had been his."

"So I wasn't hungry," growled Lonny. "That's not a crime."

Julie told them how she'd seen someone duck out of sight in the restaurant booth that night— someone who had not wanted to be seen. And later she had seen Lonny Wu in the teahouse, wearing the same green sweater he had on now, and asking Ivy if her grandmother had another Green Hornet figurine like the one he'd left behind.

"I like the Green Hornet," protested Lonny. "Big deal."

"So just now, I realized how it all fit together!" Julie raised her voice and continued. "I realized you had a good look at the coaching note when Ivy asked you to help translate it. You read that a doll was supposed to bring riches. Then later you heard Ivy's grandmother telling us about a jade necklace that her mother hadn't sent along after all. Everybody knows you're the smartest kid in Chinese school—so I guess it isn't such a surprise that you figured out before we did that the necklace could be inside the doll."

Lonny didn't say anything. He just stared sullenly at Julie.

"The problem was you didn't know what kind of doll you were looking for. So when you sneaked upstairs to the apartment, you took the only two dolls you found. You must have tucked them inside that backpack you carry around. But later, when you popped off the dolls' heads and there wasn't any necklace inside, you just threw them away."

"That was so mean!" Ivy scowled at Lonny.

"You tossed Ivy's doll in the trash behind the

restaurant that same night. But you must have kept mine to look at later, because you chucked her away behind the Chinese school."

Lonny shifted his gaze to the floor and shook his head. "You can't prove anything."

Julie took a deep breath and continued. "Then you heard us talking to Mr. Long at the teahouse about how we were trying to find Mei Meng. So you decided to track her down first and try to find the doll. Your mom was waiting on Ivy's grandparents' table the afternoon we came to the teahouse to tell everybody how we'd located Mei Meng by searching old newspaper announcements, and how we'd even talked to her son on the phone. So your mom must have told you the news, and you decided to go to Oakland yourself to see if Mei had the old doll."

Lonny shuffled his feet uncomfortably. "Nobody can prove a thing," he muttered. "You're just making it all up."

Julie glared at him. "We're not making up a single thing, and you know it! I bet you were surprised when we came to get Mrs. Liu's

library books—you raced out of there so fast.
Thank goodness we interrupted you, or you
might have pulled the heads off all her antique
dolls! But guess what, Lonny? We found Mei
first, and she had the doll with her!"

"Big deal," he muttered.

"It *was* a big deal," Julie replied. "You were
right—inside the old doll was a valuable jade
necklace!"

Lonny's shoulders sagged.

"And then," Julie continued, "we were at the
convalescent hospital, and Ivy was looking for a
pen in her grandmother's purse, and she pulled
out the Green Hornet figurine. When I saw the
figurine again, I remembered how you'd said
you wanted it. And I remembered how you
were upset that your dad lost his job. I realized
you had a reason for wanting money."

"But you must have known it wasn't right to
steal it!" Ivy added.

Lonny shrugged. "I didn't steal anybody's
money! And I didn't steal any old necklace,
either. But it's not really stealing at all if you

take something that nobody else even knows is missing."

"It is *too* stealing," Julie said staunchly.

"Well, you can't pin it on me. And anyway, it's not really breaking and entering if people leave their places unlocked in the first place."

"My mother's door was not unlocked," Mr. Liu said sternly. "I carefully locked it myself when I took her to the hospital."

"Yeah, but the window—" Lonny blurted out, and then he broke off abruptly.

There was a long silence as his words hung in the air. "So you *did* do it," said Julie. "Because how else would you know the window was unlocked?"

Now Lonny looked as if he was fighting back tears. "All right!" he muttered. "I'm sorry. But I didn't take anything!"

"Only because you didn't find what you were looking for," said Julie.

Shamefaced, Lonny looked away.

Mr. Liu marched Lonny to the office to phone his parents. Julie and Ivy slipped back through the double doors to the gym. As the disco music engulfed her, Julie found herself feeling sorry for Lonny, whose worries about his family's finances had gotten him into big trouble.

But now she could finally celebrate that the jade necklace had been brought out of hiding and rejoice in Po Po's reconnection with her dear friend—almost a sister!—after fifty years.

When the last dance was announced, Julie saw her mom standing with Olivia Kaminsky, watching the dancers. She headed over to them. Mom put her arm around Julie's shoulders. "You look tired," Mom said, and Julie nodded.

She would tell them about Lonny later. Right now she found herself looking forward to eating late-night fondue and getting to know Olivia Kaminsky. *So many people,* Julie realized, *arrive as unwelcome intruders but end up, somehow, belonging.*

Julie smiled at their visitor. "Ready to go home?" she asked.

LOOKING BACK

A PEEK INTO THE PAST

These well-dressed children were photographed on Angel Island. They were part of the merchant class, just as Ivy's grandmother was.

When Julie and Ivy were growing up, visitors to Angel Island State Park could enjoy miles of scenic trails, sandy beaches, and a narrated tram ride that circled the island in San Francisco Bay. Yet for many Chinese Americans, the words "Angel Island" brought back painful memories of immigrating to America.

Chinese immigrants first came to America in the late 1840s, during the California Gold Rush.

Like other immigrants, the Chinese saw America as a land of opportunity and eventually hoped to return home to their villages and families with newfound riches. Some did find riches, but most found only difficult and dangerous work with few rewards. In the 1860s, thousands of Chinese men were hired to help build the transcontinental railroad. Although many died from explosions and cave-ins, Chinese workers were determined to do their jobs well. Their bosses soon came to prize their work above all others'.

Chinese railroad workers blasted tunnels through mountains or hand-chiseled through granite so hard that it broke their tools.

A Chinese family in traditional dress

Still, Chinese people's customs and appearance were very different from those of most other Americans, and the Chinese often had to endure insults and physical violence. Racial prejudice against the Chinese grew until finally the government passed the Chinese Exclusion Act of 1882, which prohibited Chinese laborers from entering the United States. The act marked the first time that the United States barred a group of immigrants from entering the country because of race and class.

The law did allow certain Chinese people—

This man's identity card shows he was part of the merchant class and could legally enter the United States.

merchants, teachers, students, and diplomats—to come into the country, however. Relatives of merchants and native-born citizens could apply for admission as well. Ivy's grandmother was allowed to immigrate legally to America because her father was a merchant.

Chinese people desperate for a better life for themselves or their children did find ways around the unfair exclusion laws. Some Chinese paid legal U.S. immigrants to claim children as family members. Like Mei in Julie's story, these children were known as "paper sons" or "paper daughters." On the voyage to America, they studied coaching notes written about their "paper families" in order to memorize details about the family's village life back in China and their new lives in America.

Paper sons and daughters kept coaching notes hidden from authorities.

U.S. immigration officials at Angel Island were wary of Chinese people claiming the right to enter America. They questioned the

Women and children in a detention area of Angel Island, awaiting questioning

hopeful immigrants extensively—sometimes asking over 100 detailed questions—and compared their answers to those given by the U.S. family and other witnesses. If answers didn't match or seemed suspicious, an immigrant could be *deported*, or sent back, to China.

Those traveling from China to the port of San Francisco were *detained*, or held, on Angel Island until their papers and claims could be processed. Accessible only by ferry,

Children as young as three years old were questioned separately from their parents.

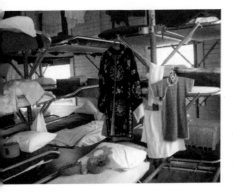

The overcrowded women's barracks had no chairs or places to store clothing.

the island was considered escape-proof. A Chinese woman who arrived in 1922 recalled, "I kept thinking in my heart, 'What a worthless trip coming here! It's like being in jail!'"

Most detainees spent several weeks on the island. Those with complicated cases spent months awaiting the outcome of their hearings. To pass time and vent frustrations, many Chinese carved poems on the walls of the barracks. Many of the poems spoke of the poor conditions and injustices endured on Angel Island.

Those detained on Angel Island were allowed outside only a few hours a day.

The Immigration Station officially closed after a disastrous fire in 1940. A few years later, the Exclusion Act was repealed, and more Chinese people were

One of over 200 poems discovered at Angel Island

allowed to enter the United States. A new law in 1965 finally opened America's borders to all Chinese immigrants.

Much of Angel Island became a state park in 1963. Some buildings were abandoned and left to deteriorate, including the barracks where many Chinese had been detained during the exclusion years. Demolition of the buildings was set to begin in 1970, until a park ranger noticed the Chinese poems inscribed on the walls.

Dale Ching tours the restored barracks at Angel Island, where he was detained for more than three months in 1937.

The Chinese American community succeeded in saving the buildings as a part of their history, and former immigrants like Po Po began to share their important and poignant stories.

Visitors who travel to Angel Island today can learn more about the immigration experiences and detainments that took place there and walk among the buildings where Chinese immigrants like Jiao Jie and Mei Meng anxiously awaited permission to enter America in search of a better life.

The Angel Island Immigration Station today

About the Author

Kathryn Reiss was a girl not much older than Julie in the 1970s. She always loved reading mysteries and started writing them herself because nothing mysterious ever seemed to happen in her own neighborhood! Her previous novels of suspense have won many awards. She teaches creative writing at Mills College and lives near San Francisco with her husband and five children.

Author's Note

Many thanks to Gene Moore and Alejandro de Jesus at the San Francisco Public Library for their invaluable information and generous help. Special thanks are also due to Casey Lee and the excellent tour guides at the Immigration Station on Angel Island, whose fascinating interpretation of history brings the past vividly to life.